ROYAL CORONATION

Printed in the United States of America: First Printing, 2023
ISBN 978-1-959981-02-2 (eBook)
ISBN 978-1-959981-03-9 (paperback)

http://www.hannahwillow217.wordpress.com

Editors: Wes Imrisek and Angela Grimes
Copy Editor: Elizabeth Daly
Cover Art: Getcovers.com
Formatting: R. L. Davennor

CHAPTER 1

"**M**r. Collins, can I use the computer?"

Casimir looked up at the man that wasn't his father, and his body shook. He tried to stand tall, but he didn't know this man well enough; it'd only been a few weeks. There hadn't been any physical punishments, but one never knew.

"Casimir, I've told you over a dozen times since you were dropped off at our house, you are not to touch the electronics. They are for real family only. Keep your sticky hands off anything in the den or we'll send you back to where you came from."

Casimir backed away from his latest foster dad. 'Where he came from' was the streets. He'd been in this house for two weeks, and so far it was one of the worst.

No, the home two homes ago was worse. So far I haven't been hit and I get fed…most nights. I don't know why anyone becomes a foster family; not one that I've been left with seems to want kids.

He went to the small room he'd been assigned. He shared it with another boy, but that kid was out. The room had two small beds, two small dressers, and a closet. The closet was empty; neither of them had enough to fill more than a drawer of the dresser.

Casimir dug in his bag for the paper.

Earlier that day, the King of Ixica came to the school with an announcement. The palace was building a new pool and they wanted a kid to design it. The King—or maybe the King and Queen together—had created a competition, and the prize was a scholarship to any college, all four years paid for.

This was Casimir's one chance for more. An escape from the streets. His parents died in a car accident while out on a date when he was six. He'd been home with a sitter; it was the last night he remembered being happy. They'd played games, had dinner, and were watching a movie when the call came in. His life had ended that night, three years ago.

He'd been placed in the system. He kept being shifted from home to home. Even at a young age, he knew the likelihood of him getting far in life was low. If he could do this one thing, design a pool for the royal family, then maybe, just maybe…

He pulled out a piece of paper and drew a rectangle. *There, a pool.*

Gazing at it, he figured it wasn't enough, but for the life of him, he couldn't think of what more would be part of a 'pool' than a hole in the ground filled with water. He'd been agonizing over it since he'd left school. In his nine years of life, he'd only gone to the city pool once, and it had been a box with water…and seats. He added smaller rectangles to represent the seats.

This was why he needed to get on the computer. He wanted to look up what fancy people had for a pool besides a hole in the ground, but Mr. Collins would never let him near anything worth any amount of money.

Clenching his jaw with determination, Casimir grabbed his bag and headed out the door. It was late, but the family wouldn't miss him if he wasn't at the table for dinner. The rules of the house stated that if he wasn't there, he didn't eat. Well, it wouldn't be the first time he'd miss a meal.

The library was less than a mile away. When he entered, the librarian smiled. "Can I help you?"

"Do you have a computer I could use, or a book on swimming pools of the rich?"

Her eyes twinkled. "You are the first to think to come here, you know. Such a brilliant young man. There's a line of computers in the center of the room with log-in information. Go start searching, and I'll bring you some examples I have that may help."

Casimir sat and searched for pools. He found images of public pools, but they didn't look much different than what he already had. He typed in 'rich pools' and he had a feeling the images he got were beyond what the palace wanted. Indoor pools the size of the school, outdoor pools in the shape of guitars, two- and three- level pools. He had no idea what would happen when someone got to the edge. Lifeguards must be important to these people.

Maybe I could be a lifeguard one day…if I ever learn how to swim.

The librarian came up with a couple of magazines. "These may help. They are design magazines. One is about home design, the other is about clothes, but some of the location images could be inspirational."

He flipped through both magazines and his heart stopped. He had no idea there were such beautiful things in the world. He was momentarily lost in the fashion he saw on the pages. The models were breathtaking…but their outfits.

His hands trembled as he traced the clothing. Page after page he saw images of men and women wearing dresses that molded to their bodies; pants and shirts that highlighted the forms, colors, angles, contrasts. It all made him tremble with excitement.

I want to create this kind of art. I never knew it even existed.

He shook himself and focused on the pools. He saw many of them included hot tubs. He saw one with a covered bed for resting, and thought that was neat. And an outdoor kitchen. *I wonder if the Royal family would like that?*

He bit his lip as he flipped through the pages. *What else would they want? Privacy? A sunroom? A slide? I dunno, I'll have to sketch these things out.*

An hour later, he had a list of notes for a fancy pool design, and a new dream for his future.

CHAPTER 2

17 YEARS LATER

Tucker searched his closet for the right outfit. He'd been working at Moore Stone Industries for almost a year, and it was time to rise above the fourth floor.

During his senior year in college, he'd reported for the school's paper. He'd gone to interview one of the junior executives at Moore Stone and arrived prepared. The man was impressed and asked him out for drinks.

The one-night stand hadn't been anything Tucker wasn't used to, but the offer of a job had been. Over the unexpected dinner they'd discussed the article and Tucker had explained what he saw were areas the company was behind the times, technologically speaking.

He hadn't thought their discussion was an interview… with benefits, but apparently the man had other ideas. While he had been a student, he didn't mind the position they'd offered him in the company. But now that he'd walked the stage and held a degree, it was time for him to demand a promotion.

His phone rang. Checking the display, he saw it was Emma, one of his best friends. "Hey, Em, what's up?"

"Did you know Moore Stone Industries just opened up a half-dozen new jobs? Both Jamie and I are thinking of applying. The dream team would be together again. What do you think?"

His hand froze reaching for his champagne suit and black button-down shirt. "They have? I've been checking the site, but missed the last couple of days. I've been distracted. Both of you working with me, that would be…" He couldn't imagine. Having these two women with him every day would make going to work so much better. It was how he'd survived the bad days at college…and high school. He already spent most of his free time at work when he wasn't with them. If Emma and Jamie were there, they'd help him to disengage. "It would be amazing, Em."

"Good, I hoped you'd say that. Tell those executives to hire us."

"On it, my friend. On it."

"Today is your big day, isn't it?" Emma asked.

"It is."

"Look, Tucker, you don't always stand up for yourself. This is really big. I'm proud of you. You deserve this. Go in and show them who they have working for them. Don't take 'no' for an answer."

He let Emma's confidence wash through him. If he could channel her conviction, he thought he could take over the world.

They hung up and he took a moment to imagine a future with the three of them working together. His mood lightened as he slipped on his suit. *Dress for the job you know you deserve.*

When he got to the tall building in downtown Chicago, he took the elevator, which moved too fast for his liking, up to the top floor. He'd made an appointment to meet with the presidents, Mr. Moore and Mr. Stone, at nine.

An executive assistant led him to a conference room. A large, highly polished, cherry wood table took up most of the room. Windows that overlooked downtown Chicago took up one wall. He could see Lake Michigan sparkling in the distance. Only the top of the top in this industry could see the lake from their offices.

He sat and faced the two older men. Mr. Moore wore a charcoal suit with a white button down. His brown eyes were warm, though his face was hard. Mr. Stone dressed more casually in a light blue button down that matched his eyes, and a black and silver tie.

The side of Mr. Moore's mouth curved up in a half-smile. "Mr. Black, you asked for this meeting. We have an international call in twenty minutes, you have that long to make your case."

Tucker fought his rapidly beating heart as his body threatened to tremble. "Two weeks ago I logged into the company's intranet from home through our VPN during the evening to complete a project that needed more bandwidth than can be used during the day. Doing a quick check of the security system, I detected a hacker trying to slip in through a hole in our firewall defense. I stopped them. I reported the situation, and was told the incident would be reported up to you."

After waiting a few seconds, he decided there wasn't going to be any confirmation coming. "A few days later I did a sweep and found evidence of other attacks on the system. I created a net that would alert me if any hacker tried to attack again. I informed my supervisor, who waved off my initiative. I have stopped three more attacks in the subsequent days. Our system isn't being protected, and soon, the company will be attacked by someone who can do real damage. Your IT security department isn't being run correctly."

One of Mr. Stone's eyebrows rose. His blue eyes deep

with challenge, he asked "And what do you propose we do, Mr. Black?"

"Promote me to head of IT Security. Let me streamline the department and ensure the company's protections are where you need and want them to be to protect our assets."

Once again, Mr. Moore gave a half smile. "And why you? You're barely out of college."

"Because I'm the best. I've stopped four attacks already and if I were the lead, your firewalls wouldn't need such micromanagement. If I had a team to train, there would be more than one person whose abilities were protecting your interests. Not to mention, the base security would be tight enough to stop most of the hackers I've seen so far."

Mr. Stone looked at his watch. "Well, our next meeting starts in four minutes." Tucker's heart dropped. He'd done what he could. "Go to HR; we'll give them a call on our way. You'll get keys to your new office." He turned to Mr. Moore. They nodded at each other. "You'll have a three month probationary window in this position, Mr. Black. Prove to us this is the right fit."

The two men stood and walked out. Tucker sat as his body trembled. He couldn't believe he'd done it. He'd fought for a new job and landed it.

CHAPTER 3

The walk between Casimir's boutique, Ixica Couture, and the palace didn't take long. He thought about the four years he'd been a small business owner and his need to pay back the King and Queen for the generosity of their loan. He'd been nervous coming to ask them for a loan. They'd already paid his way through college because of the scholarship he'd won. But once again they'd shown their belief in their people.

Once he'd delivered this last payment, he could use the extra money he'd earned each month to start saving for a car.

I wish my parents could see me now. I've gone from a street-

rat to a respectable member of Ixican society. I own my own business, and soon my own car. Maybe I'll even think about moving out of the small apartment above the work space.

Who would have guessed that the boy who practically grew up in the streets and alleys of this fair city would one day be the designer to the Royals? He thought back to the ceremony the school held when they announced the winner. His small body shivered as the King of Ixica shook his hand and patted his back.

After winning, Casimir worked to improve his grades and assemble a portfolio. Eventually, he won a spot at the Accademia Del Lusso in Italy. He felt like an imposter, but worked his ass off to graduate with honors.

When he returned to Ixica, he'd found a neglected and abandoned space he envisioned as his future shop. He'd gone with his proverbial tail between his legs to petitioned the King and Queen with the idea of a fashion store and studio.

The King's words had warmed a spot he hadn't realized needed filling. "Son, you designed a beautiful pool area for us, graduated with honors, and have returned to us instead of heading off to a more affluent center of fashion. We'll lend you the money with a system for paying us back, and you'll become an icon of fashion for Ixica."

He still preened at how proud the King had been of him and his accomplishments. No one had been satisfied with his work or with him since his parents' death.

He'd planned on taking apprentices, helping them build their own brand as well as advancing his own. They gave him the space with the agreement that he pay them off in ten years.

The upstairs had enough space for a bedroom and a combination living room/kitchen. Though he splurged for a queen sized bed, the main living space wasn't big enough for anything larger than a loveseat and a basic kitchenette. But the space was his. It was the first time in memory he'd lived alone. It took a few weeks for him to settle enough to be able to sleep through the nights.

The remodeling took longer than he'd hoped. The storefront had been his first priority, and within a few weeks he displayed some of the works he'd designed in school. People bought them up and even commissioned him to create more before his studio was completed. He worked from the tiny flat above the store, sometimes pulling all-nighters to get jobs done.

It had taken work, but his business had taken off, the people in town loved his designs. He couldn't believe how successful he'd been. After this trip to see the scary advisor of the King and Queen, Master Sidney, the store would be all his.

As he ascended the steps, the grand doors opened. One of the myriad staff greeted him. "Mr. Silk, here to see Master Sidney?"

"Yes, please. I have an appointment scheduled with him at eleven."

"I'll take you to a conference room and let him know you're here."

His heart pounded. He tried to hold himself aloof, but the palace intimidated him. Even the palace staff, all uniformed in plum slacks and black coats, were dressed in fabrics richer than half of what he could stock in his store. The rugs and tapestries on the walls—he couldn't imagine the history behind each piece. He could sit and draw, inspired by any corner of the lush building.

Shaking himself, he focused on following the nice young woman who led him up the grand staircase. He kept waiting to be kicked out as unworthy, but they always accepted him. Everyone was so warm and welcoming.

In the conference room they offered him tea and biscuits. He didn't have to wait long for Master Sidney to arrive. "Mr. Silk," Sidney said as he swept into the room with his chin lifted, staring down his nose at Casimir.

Well, most *of the people are warm and welcoming.*

Before he could say anything, the Queen herself entered, and the two of them took seats on the opposite side of the table. Casimir tensed every muscle in his body to stop himself from shaking. He forced his legs to straighten as he stood and bowed. "Your Majesty, Master Sidney, thank you for joining me. I didn't expect to see you both."

The Queen smiled brightly. "Oh, sit, Mr. Silk. I just wanted to come and tell you how proud we are. I understand that this is your last payment, and the store is yours. You've paid everything off early, too. Lovely."

Mouth suddenly dry, Casimir just nodded. He sipped his tea, hoping that would help. "Thank you, Your Majesty. It thrills me every day to work in fashion, and it wouldn't have happened without you and the King."

"Good, good. Now, the King and I have a formal dinner with some dignitaries. I need a new dress. Silver, or maybe charcoal gray. Champagne accents. I'll need it by next week."

Casimir's brain stopped working for a few seconds. If he started designing for the Queen, there'd be no end to what he could do.

CHAPTER 4

PRESENT DAY

Tucker's mind wandered as he spun in his high-backed leather chair. The cerulean sky dotted with white fluffy clouds outside his window reminded him of *The Simpsons* TV show right before the words erupted from behind the building skyline. His office with the drab tan walls and generic desert tapestry didn't excite him as much as the idea of being outdoors. Round and round he went, his eyes scanning the blue sky, then the tan walls, as he debated his options.

He loved his job, when there was work to do. He excelled at what he did; it was how he'd earned an office with a view of Lake Michigan. What his friends Emma and Jamie didn't know was, when he wasn't in the office, he did a lot of work from home.

His head started to pound, so he stopped the spinning and placed his hands on his smooth, oak desk. He'd finished off all his loose-end projects and got the rest of his responsibilities moved over to his people in advance of his three-week vacation. The company wasn't happy that he'd left for two weeks for Jamie's wedding, and now he planned to leave again. Human resources told him it wouldn't be fully paid, but he agreed to the stipulation. He saved a large part of his salary each month, not having many monetary needs. He knew it would be harder for Emma, but he offered to help if she needed it.

Tucker stood and took a final circuit of his office, slipping any trinket that he felt was personal into his briefcase. There wasn't much chance that someone would enter his office and steal his property, but he wanted to plan for any contingency… including the one where he stood up for himself, was strong, and followed his heart. He'd done that once, but he wasn't sure he could do it again. He could dream.

The elevator whizzed him down to Emma's floor. The speed always made his head spin, but having an office on a lower floor equated to a demotion. Floor height in this company meant respect and a larger paycheck.

Emma's desk was a study in archaeological wonder. He

gazed at the layers of coffee mugs, papers, and knick knacks, and wondered how she ever got anything done. He knew she did, but never understood how. She was the most organized, efficient worker, but on first impression she was pure chaos.

Her head popped up and she gave him a big smile. "Is it time? Are we finally heading out? I am *so* excited!"

One…two…three…

"I'm just going to send a quick text to Adrian that we're leaving in ten minutes and then clean up." Emma's hand flew up with her phone.

Ever since their first trip out, she'd been obsessed with the Prince, and apparently, he was okay with her constant communication. The two had been texting every day. "Wow, that took almost ten seconds, Em. And you can get that—" He waved his hand towards her desk, "—organized in ten minutes?"

Her eyes narrowed in challenge, and his best friend morphed into a Tasmanian devil. Tucker checked his watch and then watched in utter bafflement as the desk covered in inches of stuff evaporated. He shook his head when, in eight and a half minutes, her desk was clear. She skipped off and came back with a wet wipe and gave her desk a final cleaning, giving Tucker an imperial smirk she'd need to teach Jamie.

Emma slipped her arm in Tucker's and dragged him to the elevator. The box dropped them to the lobby and they retreated from the company's building. Once outside, Emma turned to him. "Okay, we'll each head home, get our bags, and meet at the airport. *Adrian,*" she said the name with a sigh, "said he'd have the royal airplane waiting for us."

God, she's practically swooning. How long will I have to put up with this?

He pulled her in to kiss each of her cheeks and turned to walk away. Their routes home took them in opposite directions.

"Excuse me, sir, and ma'am." A voice from the road caught his attention. He spun on his heel. Emma stopped, too. A man in a black tux and a fancy hat stared at them. "I was ordered to ensure Lady Emma Rhett and Lord Tucker Black arrived at the airport in a timely manner. From the description, I believe that would be the two of you. May I facilitate your passages?"

Tucker rolled his eyes and chuckled. "Is this what happens when you're besties with a prince?"

Emma had the decency to blush. "Honestly, I had no idea." She reached over and took his hand, dragging him to the open back door. "Being royalty must be amazing. You know it could've just as easily been Jamie. She knows us and the job better than Adrian does."

Once they were in the car and belted, Tucker gave the driver directions to his apartment. It was closer to downtown Chicago than Emma's place and made more sense as the first stop. Emma grabbed her phone and started texting. Tucker did a few updates on social media and then shut his phone. He wasn't really in the mood. Emma was still engrossed in her conversation when they arrived at his small walkup.

Tucker told the driver to wait as he ran up and dropped off his work bag and replaced it with his two suitcases. He did one last check of his refrigerator and bathroom to make sure there was nothing that would surprise him when… if?…he returned.

He loved Emma, but she didn't need him here. She had family and friends and could survive anywhere. *The question is…can I do it? Am I strong enough to follow my heart despite the fear I'm feeling?*

The driver secured his items in the trunk and they headed to Emma's larger, nicer, apartment. It was farther from downtown and less expensive. It also took her three times as long to get anywhere.

She finally emerged from her phone. "Jamie sent the car. She thought it would make our escape from work and Chicago easier. I guess she's excited to see us…or something," Emma said jokingly then began to bounce, too much energy packed into her petite body.

The stop at her place took a bit longer. Tucker and the driver waited in silence while Emma finished doing whatever it was she needed to do.

Sitting and waiting, Tucker thought about friends and

family. Unlike Emma and Jamie, he didn't have family to distract him from working his way up the company ladder. And that was the heart of his issue: what kept him in Chicago? Why didn't he find something more challenging?

Once Emma's door swung open, the driver lept out and helped her load her luggage into the trunk and then they were off to the airport and the long flight. He wondered again if he had the strength to make this trip his last.

CHAPTER 5

Casimir watched Malcolm and Finley walk out of his office and sighed. The two were stunning together. After he designed their wedding, everyone would see how beautiful the next Kings of Ixica were.

Who would have guessed that the boy who practically grew up in the streets and alleys of this fair city would one day be the designer to the Royals?

So few people know how much impact a small action, a kind word, or a bit of encouragement could do in the life of a child. The Royal family of Ixica always did this for their people, and he wanted to make sure he could express his gratitude to them. Designing their royal wedding was such a small thing.

Casimir shook his head, dismissing his memories. He had a few hours to get some sketches down before he went to the palace to have dinner with the Queen. Just thinking about it made his heart beat faster. He'd had a few interactions with her in the prelude to Princess Anastasia's wedding, but meeting with her never grew mundane.

He made a board of what he wanted to create and then asked his lead assistant, Tabatha, to compile a few sketches and put it in a leather satchel while he went and changed. He slipped up to his flat and placed his wallet, keys, and phone on the table for two in the corner.

Searching through his clothes, he decided on night-blue slacks with a cream button-down shirt and a matching tie. Formal, but not over the top. He made sure his curls were still styled before he headed down to grab the portfolio. Outside his shop, he found his model S Tesla in its parking spot. He'd had it wrapped in the plum color of his nation.

When he pulled into the palace's circular drive, he parked where the security staff indicated and stepped from his car, listening for the beep that told him the car was locked as he walked away.

As he approached the stairs up to the main door, he saw a bedraggled couple. The woman was petite with fiery red hair and the man had blond curls that framed his face like a fresco painting. He was beautiful. *A shame he is with that woman.* Despite looking tired, he still looked put-together in black slacks and a tailored light gray shirt.

The servant at the door smiled at him as he approached. "Oh, Mr. Silk, I can lead all three of you up to the family dining room together. This is perfect. You remember Lady Emma Rhett and Lord Tucker Black from the wedding?"

Casimir took a closer look at the two people and had a vague memory of them being the ones to stand up with the American Princess.

The man looked pained. "Why does everyone call us 'Lady' and 'Lord'?"

The servant bowed her head. "Prince Adrian asked us to, of course, and the Princess Jamie agreed. This way, please."

Lord Tucker rubbed his eyes, which Casimir couldn't help but notice matched his shirt perfectly. Casimir thought he heard him mutter something about throttling a Princess who'd gotten too big for her britches.

Once they'd made it to the dining room, Lady Emma was seated next to Prince Adrian, and they both blushed, smiling and talking quietly. Lord Tucker was placed next to Princess Jamie. The two hugged and spoke as fast as any two Americans. Thankfully, Casimir was given the honor of sitting to the right of the Queen herself, who of course sat at the head of the table. He knew that nothing would be discussed until after the meal, but again he marveled at how far he'd come in his short life.

Once the last plate was cleared away, the Queen smiled at her family and guests. "Shall we retire to the guest family room? It's recently been cleaned."

To his left, Malcolm and Finley groaned in unison and Prince Adrian laughed. Casimir didn't know the story, but he figured he could get it later from Malcolm. He missed having the man around regularly, both as a designer and a friend.

They all stood and headed up to the third floor room. The Princesses sat together on one of the loveseats, and Malcolm and Finley took the other. Prince Adrian, Lady Emma, and Lord Tucker took a couch. That left the single seats for the Queen and Casimir.

Prince Adrian and Lady Emma continued to flirt, leaving Lord Tucker to sit looking like a third wheel. Casimir reevaluated his initial assumption. As he presented his plans for the days leading up to the wedding, he kept his eyes on the Queen and Malcolm and a bit on Finley, to see what they all thought. But from the corner of his eyes, he watched this blond American.

The uncomfortable Lord Tucker watched Casimir, not his presentation, but him. The man's legs and arms were crossed and his shoulders were tight. He looked like he needed to sit in the Royal hot tub. *Do not think of that man in just a swimsuit!*

Casimir had done enough presentations, especially wedding plan presentations, that it required only half his attention, leaving the rest free to piece together who this stranger was and what his role would be at the palace.

When he finished, he gave a slight bow to the Queen. "Your Majesty, do you have any questions? Any items you'd like me to add or take away?"

Malcolm snorted. "Really Casimir, you don't ask me and Finley? It's *our* wedding."

He raised an eyebrow. "I may consult you, friend, but not that man you're marrying. He's pretty to look at, but I've heard his opinions. I'll give him no say in this event… or any future ones, if I can have my way."

Finley threw his head back and laughed. Something in Casimir relaxed that he'd made a future King laugh with his impertinence. He saw the America's jaw drop in shock, but Prince Adrian laughed just as hard. "Well, Fin, he has your number. No pockets or cargo shorts at any events for you!"

Lord Tucker leaned forward to see Lord Finley. "You want to wear cargo pants at your wedding? I mean, I'm American, known for…well, being American, and even I know better than that."

Finley's eyes narrowed. "Tucker, you may be American, but you're a fashion gay, a regular gay metrosexual, and I'm not. I'm a dying breed. I like men *and* comfortable clothing.

You should take notes from me."

The other man laughed. "If that means cargo shorts, I'll pass. I can be comfortable and stylish. How does Prince Malcolm put up with you?"

Malcolm turned to the American. "Fire…a nightly ritual if you must know. You should join me; we'll make s'mores!"

Falling back on the couch, Lord Tucker's face transformed as he laughed and for a moment Casimir's breath caught. Casimir enjoyed listening to the banter, but he knew he should finish up his presentation. "So, *besides pockets*, are there any other additions?"

The Queen tilted her head. "What about the coronation?"

CHAPTER 6

After the plane ride and the trip to the palace, Tucker wanted to enjoy his food, but there were too many distractions. First, there was Jamie. He was dying to hear everything about her honeymoon.

"Tomorrow!" she whispered. "We'll all sit poolside, drink mimosas, and gossip. It will be wonderful."

Then there was Emma who was knee-deep in intrigue with Prince Adrian. The two of them looked ready to elope. He wondered if anyone else realized how close the two had become since they'd first met. *Do either of them realize there are others at the table?*

Finally, and worst of all, was the man who'd entered with them, Mr. Silk. He thought he recognized the man from their last visit, but he wasn't sure, they'd met so many people during Jamie's wedding. This man was spectacular, how could he *not* remember him specifically? Not a hair out of place. His outfit was immaculate. The way he walked, how he stood, even the way he spoke to the Queen, was entrancing. Tucker felt like a country bumpkin next to him, but he wanted to be next to him anyway.

He kept darting glances at the designer, trying not to get caught. If his plan were to work, he needed to get his head on straight, and that didn't involve being head over heels for the first hot man he saw. *Focus, Tucker; see your goal, meet with Malcolm and Finley, see if you can get a job, and* then *lose your freaking mind. You know this country feels more like home than Chicago ever did; don't lose track of what you want to do here.*

Tucker wasn't even sure what had been served for dessert as his plate was whisked away. All his focus had been on Mr. Silk. He followed the others up the stairs to the guest living room. He ended up behind Mr. Silk and couldn't help appreciating the fit of his dark blue pants. *God above, man. Are you in high school? He's just a man— sexy, yes—but you've seen plenty of attractive men in your life.*

He sat beside Emma on a couch with Prince Adrian. On the other side of the Prince sat the soon to be Kings,

Prince Malcolm and Lord Finley. They were laughing at some joke and Tucker smiled at their amusement. On his other side, seated upon another small couch, was Jamie and her new wife. It made him happy seeing the two of them together. He never thought Jamie was unhappy in her previous relationships, but Star made her *happy*. And he hoped Jamie brough Star just as much joy.

Tucker leaned towards the newest Princess. "Can you explain this 'Lord' business? I'm lost every time someone says 'Lord Tucker.'"

Jamie winked at him. "That was Adrian's idea. He thought it would make it easier for you and Emma to move around the palace and city if you each had a title. You should've seen the ceremony that we had with the Queen to get your name on the books."

The presentation was almost fully set up. He rubbed his eyes, trying to contemplate a meeting with all the Royals to assign titles to him and Emma. He slid his eyes back over to Emma. "So, is the title legitimate? Like, really official? There's no getting around this malarkey? You had a ceremony?"

"Right as rain. You are a Lord of Ixica, Tucker. If you don't calm your shit, I'll arrange for you to acquire an estate. So, suck it up, and stop complaining. I have to deal with people calling me 'Princess' and 'Your Highness.' We all have to adjust."

Before he could answer, Mr. Silk began his presentation

of the wedding plans. Most of the information was lost on Tucker as he watched the presenter instead of the minutiae on the boards. At the end, Lord Finley's desire for pockets cracked him up and he relaxed for the first time since arriving at the palace.

The next day after breakfast, he slid into his designer swimsuit. It was bright blue, tight, and just covered all the bits that needed covering. He'd gone out with Emma to buy a new suit the previous weekend, and he'd debated getting the longer shorts. Emma had refused, saying this one was much better. At least the pool was private.

He arrived before the girls and decided to get in a few laps. Once the others made it, they all slid into the hot tub. He was happy to see Princess Anastasia had joined them.

Emma leaned back in the heat. "Okay ladies, spill. I want all the gossip on your trip to the islands. I've always wanted to visit Hawaii."

The two spent some time describing the islands and their time in paradise, but all too soon, Jamie leaned forward, eyes narrow, and demanded, "What is happening between you and Adrian?"

Princess Anastasia laughed. "I haven't seen my brother so distracted since he was in college. Spill."

Tucker watched Emma squirm, so he poked her with his toe. "Yeah, Emma, tell the Princesses about how long the two of you have been texting. Have you ever gone a full hour without checking in since you've met him?"

Suddenly, he was in the spotlight; all three of them stared at him. Princess Anastasia's brow slowly rose. "Okay, I'm guessing you didn't get the message because you're in a different room—not one of the gals—so we'll go over this once. Call me Anastasia…Star, if you really want, but no titles unless we're in public. They're obnoxious, especially when we're in a hot tub together. The same goes for my brothers. As for the Queen…you'll have to work that out with her."

His whole body felt cold despite the warmth of the water. "I'm sorry…er…Anastasia. Are you sure? No titles at all? I don't want to offend anyone, and the first thing that happened to me when your driver picked me up, was he called me by a title. I'm new to all this…" He stopped talking when he realized he'd been babbling.

Jamie shook her head. "And did you like it, doofus?"

He sank down until only his head was above the water. "Well, honestly…no."

The three laughed, and once he thought about it, he joined in.

After they got that straightened out, they all turned back to Emma, who blushed, then snorted. "I don't know what's between me and Adrian. He's handsome and nice…

and apparently likes me. It's a great combination. We're just trying to figure things out right now. He's mostly busy with training Finley and Malcolm." She turned to Anastasia. "Shouldn't you be helping with that, too?"

She shrugged. "Eventually, but I got away before Sidney found me to give me a schedule. And if he had, I'd have just explained that you two had just shown up, and as my wife's best friends and family, it's my duty to help welcome you and make you feel comfortable. I think my duty here is clear. As a Royal Princess, I must sit and gossip in the hot tub!"

Before they could say more, the door opened and Prince Malcolm sauntered out…grr! Malcolm, *just* Malcolm. *Figure this out, Tucker, figure this out!* He came up to the hot tub and smiled. "Look at you, my man, in a hot tub full of women. Every man's dream, right?"

Emma and Jamie choked back laughter and Tucker slowly checked Malcolm out head to foot in his most provocative way he could. The man was engaged, but he was pretty. "I think it would be more like a dream with you and Finley, but not more fun." Malcolm winked at Tucker's over the top flirting as Tucker continued, "Watching the two of you without having someone of my own is never as much fun as one may think. Alas, the single life seems to be my lot in life." He shrugged before turning back towards the others.

Emma smiled, a bit sadly. Jamie reached under the water to give his knee a squeeze.

From behind him, Malcolm laughed. "My good bitch, well said! I can't help you with your dating woes, but I do wonder, could I trouble you to do a job for us?"

Excited at the prospect, he turned back with a smile. "I can probably find time in my very busy schedule… though, you know…swimming pool, tanning. What did you have in mind?"

"We need a liaison with the designer, Casimir. The man you met last night."

CHAPTER 7

Three of the five boards for the wedding were complete. Casimir debated how much of a cross-over he wanted to make from the wedding to the coronation. The two events would be separated by time, so they didn't have to match completely. The suits for the wedding would be charcoal, but the coronation…that wasn't a commitment between the two men, it was a vow they'd be making to the people of Ixica. The presentation and symbolism needed to be larger.

He headed into the storage room and collected a selection of materials to scrutinize for use in the second ceremony. He hadn't decided his final direction, but he often got inspiration from the fabric itself.

Casimir put pencil to paper and shut his eyes, imagining the day the two men became Kings of Ixica. What did he want to see, smell, feel, experience? As a spectator in the audience, what would make the day exceptional for him? He let his mind wonder, playing around with different scenarios.

His fingers explored the fabrics, letting it add texture to the mental landscape, the stories playing out in his mind. Each time his hand moved, the scene he saw morphed. He could lose himself in this type of rumination as his prep for a big celebration took shape.

The door to his shop opened and Casimir pulled himself from his musings. Stepping from his workroom, he walked out to the main showroom to see who was in need of his services. There were times Tabatha or another of his assistants met with customers, but Casimir liked giving the people of Ixica his personal attention when he could. He had time at the moment.

Instead of a new customer, or even a repeat customer, Casimir found Lord Tucker, the American friend of the new Princess. He wore an immaculate pair of wine slacks and a black button down shirt with a matching black tie. The outfit was tailored. His blond curls were perfectly styled to frame his face and his gray eyes didn't waver from their focus on Casimir.

He gave a tight smile. "Mr. Silk, Prince Malcolm asked

me to serve as liaison between you and the Royal family. Everyone else seems to have a job…either that, or they were trying to subtly figure a way to ship me off for the day." He gave a winning smile. "Either way, if I can get a quick update, you can stash me in a corner until my ride comes to collect me. You'll not even know I'm here. I'm very good at disappearing and not being noticed at all."

Casimir wasn't sure if Lord Tucker knew how to blend into the background, but he smiled and tilted his head. "If you're going to be spending any time in my shop, Lord Tucker, I insist on you calling me Casimir. I get itchy every time you call me 'Mr. Silk.'" He saw the man flinch at his title, and predicted what was coming next.

The man relaxed by a degree and gave Casimir a genuine smile. Casimir lost his breath at how stunningly beautiful he was, how angelic. "I'll only drop the formality if you'll agree to call me Tucker. I don't know what got into Jamie, to decide to give me a title…I'm sorry, Princess Jamie. I probably won't be great with remembering that, just so you know. If you're offended by my slip-ups," he blushed—perfectly—and gave a small shrug, "I'm sorry. I'm trying to get better, but this is all so new to me. I know that I'll be apologizing a lot…she's been a friend of mine for years."

Casimir placed his hand on Tucker's arm and led him to the back workroom. "Tell me, Tucker, do you have any qualifications to be reporting on what I do?"

He felt the man stiffen under his hand, though there wasn't much other reaction. "None, sir. Again, I'm fairly certain they were just trying to occupy my time, give me something to do to get me out of their way."

"Well, what do you do back home; anything with fashion? You certainly know how to dress yourself."

Tucker looked down at himself and huffed out a laugh. "Mr., er, I mean, Casimir, I work in tech. I'm the head of tech security and most other things that have to do with technology at the firm where I work. As for how I'm dressed—" he held out his hands. "—you were dressed so immaculately, I decided it was the least I could do to show my respect."

Casimir leaned on his desk and considered the man. "Is there something in your past that would've made the others think you knew more about fashion than you do?"

"My past?" The man's pale skin lost more of its color before he shook his head. "No, nothing in my past. I doubt Jamie would've shared anything about my past anyway. Look, let's just leave it as I'm not qualified, but all I'm doing is taking some notes and playing messenger. I'll try to stay out of your way once you give me a rundown of what you have. I'm sorry you have to work with me and not someone experienced, like Prince Malcolm."

Casimir sighed and decided to just deal with the man. "For you to understand my projects, I'd like to start by showing you my workspace." He threw out his arm. "This is my dream come true, where I create all the custom designs. The walls are both inspiration and works in progress. Ahead, through those doors, are the sewing rooms. To the left are the break room, toilets, and coat room, and to the right is the fabric room and stairs."

There were people focused on tasks in different areas, a few working on other orders, following patterns he'd created for clients. Cutting, pinning, sewing. A few off in private rooms, designing. Their work would be double checked before anything went live.

He led Tucker to his boards. "As you can see, I have three of the boards done for the wedding. I've determined what the men will wear, the style, color, fabric, and overall feel for the ceremony. I've created a selection of ideas for the page boy and flower girl, as well as ideas for the people standing up with them. I'll need more details on that before I finalize anything."

Checking over his shoulder, he noticed that Tucker had pulled out a small notebook and he took notes. His focus was entirely on the boards and Casimir's work. Casimir thought back on his presentation in the palace when Tucker seemed less focused on what was being shown and realized that this time, Tucker was working. He was impressed. "Do you have any questions?"

Tucker shook his head while taking in everything on the

table, then tilted his head to the side where four bolts of fabric lay. "Is there a plan for that selection of fabric? It's gorgeous, but doesn't seem to really match anything on these three boards. It's close, but not quite right." He blushed again. "I'm sorry, it isn't my place to judge; you're the expert." He took a half-step back as if afraid he'd been offensive.

Casimir offered him a genuine smile. He hadn't been this excited to talk shop with a stranger since Malcolm had first started challenging him. "Don't apologize; you're correct. Those are ideas I'm playing with for the coronation. I was just starting to conceptualize when you walked into my shop."

Tucker's eyes widened to saucers and he backed up another step. He licked his lips and raised his hands. "I'm really sorry to have interrupted you; find a place to stash me away and I'll be out of your hair until a palace car comes to collect me. Please, get back to doing what you need to do. I really don't want to be a bother. I'm sure I have enough to report for today."

Casimir raised his eyebrows. He enjoyed discussing his ideas with Tucker, but he was right, he wasn't qualified, and maybe wasn't comfortable with the topic. He was also no Royal; he didn't know how to play the power games. *I guess it's time to get back to work.* "You're fine, you didn't interrupt anything. I could've sent someone else to answer the door. There's an empty table over there and you're correct that I've shown you everything for now."

CHAPTER 8

Tucker sat in the corner and double-checked the notes he'd taken for Malcolm and Finley. He wasn't sure if they'd be shared with the Queen as well, but he was confident the notes included enough information to impress her if necessary. When he got home he would translate his shorthand into a typed report.

In college, he'd earned money as a court reporter for the campus newspaper. He'd learned shorthand to help take accurate notes. He'd kept up the skill for times like these when quick, accurate notes were needed. Years as a reporter gave him the ability to hone in on what a person said, getting to the heart of a matter.

Once he was satisfied he'd gotten everything down he needed, he darted a few quick glances at Casimir. He wore a black turtleneck sweater under a dark gray jacket. His black pants fit him like a glove. The man's frustration at having an interloper and keeping his back to Tucker worked for him. Tucker did *not* mind the view at all.

Not wanting to distract the artist from his work, Tucker turned back to his notebook. He knew Casimir didn't want him here. He wasn't sure he'd want anyone here, but someone as unqualified as he was definitely wouldn't be high on the designer's list.

He found a clean page and began to doodle. He started with the artist himself. He spent an hour sketching Casimir as he worked. He wasn't the best artist, but it distracted him nicely. Once he'd created a few basic sketches, he selected his favorite and fleshed it out. He only had his pencil, so it was a study in shades of gray.

After he finished the portrait of Casimir, he turned to another empty page and sketched out a new crown. There would be two Kings now, not a King and Queen, and if he were Finley, he'd want something new. He imagined a new staff with an oval twisted top that could hold a jewel. Tucker lost himself in his artwork, filling in details as he had time.

He spun and turned the images around in his mind, viewing them from different angles, and sketched the results.

When he'd been young and making costumes for himself to escape his mundane life, he'd create sketches like this, twisting each image as he imagined it from different angles.

At home, he had a computer with a sophisticated CAD program that let him play around with these designs. He'd debated packing it up before he left, but he hadn't thought he'd have much time to play on a computer. Or, maybe, he hoped he wouldn't have much time to lose himself in his computer. He glanced around the designer's studio. *I suppose I should re-evaluate the amount of free time I'll have here in Ixica.*

He rubbed his eyes, leaning down as he rested his elbow on the table. There was no need to waste anyone else's time; he'd pack up and walk back to the palace. Based on his memory, the route was fairly straight forward. And the exercise would do him some good.

Tucker picked up his book, tucking the pencil in the small elastic holder in the side, and stood, stretching. Casimir, working at the center table, spun on his heel to face him. With a half a grin, Tucker lifted his book and waved. "I think I'll walk. You're busy and I don't think anyone's coming for another hour or so. I'm not sure what they thought I'd be doing…maybe getting lessons? But I'll be off now."

Casimir's brows dropped for a minute before one lifted. "Would you like a ride?"

Tucker shook his head. "No, you're busy. Your time is worth more than mine right now. I'll be fine."

The designer tossed his pencil on the table. "Is this an American thing? The need to always be working? I'll drive you back, I wouldn't want you to get lost in our fair city. The round trip won't take but a minute, and I could use a bit of a break."

With a chuckle, Tucker acquiesced. "It may be an American thing. It may just be a 'me' thing. I don't like imposing on others. It's…well, that's a bit of a story, more than the quick drive, and probably more than you want to be dragged into hearing, let's just say…thank you."

Casimir looked down his nearly perfect nose at him and gave him a slight smile. "Well, we got there in the end; that's something."

He led Tucker to a plum Tesla, and Tucker slid into the passenger seat. The massive interface display of the Tesla always impressed him, but he clenched his fists to stop himself from playing. He rested his balled hands on his book on his lap instead.

The walk to the palace wouldn't have been hard. As soon as Casimir pulled into traffic, the palace was obvious to any idiot with eyes to see. Minutes into the ride, a biker flew out from the curb, crossing in front of the car. Casimir slammed on the brakes, his hand reaching out to push back on Tucker's belly, like a mother with a child. "Damn bikers. They have every right to the road, as long as they follow the rules like all the rest of us."

Tucker's heart pounded the rest of the way to the palace. He debated if he'd get such a great heart rate if he'd walked.

CHAPTER 9

As Casimir watched the biker disappear around the corner, he realized his hand still rested on Tucker's tight abs. Not wanting to call attention to himself, he slowly moved his hand away, though the tingling in his palm and fingers continued. He rubbed his palm stealthily with his fingers before placing his hand back on the wheel.

Next to him, Tucker's head was leaned down and his eyes were closed. "You should've just let me walk home. You almost got into an accident. I'm sorry." He finally looked up and watched the road ahead of them.

It's cute that he's worried about me, but he has to let other people do things for him. That biker wasn't his fault.

On a whim, Casimir turned left at the next intersection. Tucker frowned, his gaze bouncing between the palace, Casimir, and their new route. "Am I missing something?"

"Just a quick detour. This road loops around back to the main boulevard. We'll pass all the schools and a park. Just thought we could talk for a minute, if you're not in too much of a hurry."

Tucker's eyes widened a bit, and Casimir wasn't sure if Tucker breathed when he nodded. From the corner of his eye, he saw the man's face harden and then his mouth quirked to the side. "Talk for a minute? Huh. Firing me already, then?"

Casimir shook his head and smiled. "You're living in the palace with a title now; you need to play the part. You said you do security at your current job. You any good?"

His face softened. "Yeah, one of the youngest people on the management team in the company's history. After I was hired, I convinced them I was invaluable and if they didn't promote me they'd be idiots. After they saw what I brought to the company, they agreed."

Casimir's brow rose. From the moment he met Tucker, he'd seemed like a bit of a mouse of a man—beautiful, but introverted at best, maybe a bit socially awkward at worst. He apologized and tried to stay out of everyone's way. He couldn't imagine him demanding a promotion. "I'd like to meet that man: secure in who he is, demanding his station in life. Sounds…well, that's who you should be here."

The man's face fell into a mask of self mockery and he shrugged. "Easier said than done. I can be as arrogant as the next man when I'm in my element. The problem is, I'm not in my element here. Titled in the palace and liaison at a fashion house. Give me a computer and a goal, and I can do anything."

"Well, go after what you want here. There are lots of things happening in the palace. Figure it out. Be that arrogant manager who demanded a promotion."

Tucker sat next to him, watching out the window. Casimir took a moment as they navigated the slower side streets to appreciate how fit the man next to him was. He'd sworn years ago, after working with dozens, maybe even hundreds of married couples, he'd never do anything serious. Well, a man visiting from another country for a few weeks was as 'not serious' as they came.

I wonder if he'd be up for a romp to get the edge off. It's been too long. Everyone in town knows me, and if I were promiscuous it would damage my reputation, but Tucker… he's leaving town soon.

Casimir still wasn't completely positive the other man was interested, but the chase was half the excitement.

"You're not wrong." It took Casimir a second to catch up to what Tucker referred to. He thought back through his musings to the last thing he'd actually said aloud. "I should speak with Jamie, see if there's anything useful I can do besides lounge by that damn pool. I haven't done this much lounging…well, ever. I'm not built to live like this. I need more action."

Again, Casimir had to bite back a laugh at how much the words fit with both what he'd said out loud, and what he'd been thinking. He could give the man action if that's what he wanted.

It didn't take much longer before they pulled up to the palace. Tucker swiveled to face him and gave him a huge smile. "Thanks for the ride and mini-tour. I haven't actually seen much of Ixica beyond the palace and the airport. I guess I'll descend again in a few days. Enjoy your time off for good behavior." He waggled his brows before opening the door and sliding out. Casimir noted he didn't even need assistance with the Tesla's unique features.

Casimir watched as Tucker ascended the stairs, his tight ass flexing excellently beneath his perfectly tailored pants. Oh, yeah, this would definitely be someone worth pursuing.

CHAPTER 10

Tucker lay in his bed, arms folded behind his head, legs crossed, and gazed unseeing at his ceiling. His mind bounced between the man he found so freaking attractive and the words of wisdom he gave. Thinking about Casimir made his body tighten with need despite the man's obvious disinterest. *Focus on your goal, Tucker. Casimir's disinterest is a good thing. Focus on your goals.*

How can I show the Royal family my use to them?

He groaned as his mind spun, hitting dead-end after dead-end. He needed to learn more about the palace and what it required to be able to answer that question.

He heard his door open and before he could react, two bodies fell on him, laughing. He pushed himself onto his elbows and smiled wide at Emma and Jamie. "And to what do I owe this surprise?"

Emma slapped his chest. "We want to hear about your day with that gorgeous designer."

Tucker rolled his eyes and fell back. "You mean the Godlike arrogant one who thinks I'm an American fool unqualified to be the liaison to a designer?" He pushed up again and glared at Jamie. "Is this your doing? You know he isn't wrong. What do I know about design and fashion?"

Jamie dropped down into a cross-legged position. Emma mirrored her and, scooting back, Tucker did as well. Jamie winked. "Besides being the best-dressed man I know?" She started ticking things off on her fingers. "You always predict all the critiques when we watch the fashion shows. You've attended a fashion show in Paris with the company…once. Oh, yeah, and you're gay."

He leaned forward and lightly punched her arm. "So is your Lord Finley, and from what I understand, he wants to wear cargo shorts to his wedding. Liking men does not equate to knowing anything about fashion. As for the rest, all that doesn't fit into a resume. My resume is IT security and you know it. I feel useless. Isn't there something I can do on a computer? If I spend another day lounging around this palace of yours, my head may explode."

Jamie's eyes narrowed. "Are you sure?"

Like a wolf on the trail of a rabbit, he leaned forward, fully focused on his friend. "Talk, woman."

She bit her lower lip before scrunching up her face. "Okay, here's the deal. I've been given my first project. Finley and I are creating a new computer security system." Tucker sat upright, watching Jamie. "The palace's system is horrible, from what I can tell. We think we'll need to hire some people. Neither of us have done that sort of thing before…wanna help?"

He launched at her, engulfing her in a hug. "God above, please, yes, and thank you! You know that's my specialty—all of it! Hell, hire me." Sitting back, bubbles of doubt assailed him and he slapped his hands over his mouth, eyes widening.

Emma's mouth dropped open. "Is this why you've been so weird? You don't want to return to Chicago?"

Tucker slumped. "To be honest, yes. I have nothing there but you and my job. The idea of starting over new is so seductive. This country, it calls to my bones. I don't even know much about it, but I'd love to stay and give it a go. I just…I don't have much and I can't come without a job. I just hoped…" He shrugged, not knowing how to finish his thoughts.

Jamie smiled. "Well, tomorrow morning, after breakfast, we'll meet with Finley about building an IT department focused on maintaining a network and creating a security system worthy of you, my friend."

He dressed carefully the next morning…again. He suddenly realized he may not have packed enough despite his two overpacked suitcases. Friendly, relaxed, but a possibility for a job interview. Not too desperate, but professional. He needed to impress Finley, but not look like he was trying… even though that was exactly what he was doing. *I want this so damn badly, but I can't let everyone know. If I keep pulling at my hair, I'll go down there bald!*

Tucker dug through his suitcase until he found a pair of dark-wash jeans and a gray long-sleeve t-shirt that matched his eyes with the words 'Get past this wall' engulfed in flames. He wore it when he worked during off-hours. It had been a gift from Emma and he'd planned on wearing it on the flight home. Soft and comforting, he hoped it worked for the day on two levels.

Jamie and Finley met him in the family dining room. He'd miss the food if and when he was kicked out of the palace. Today's offerings were a soft-boiled egg embedded in a roll topped with butter. There were sweet jams and honey, slices of different meats and cheese, and fresh fruit. And of course…coffee. The staff explained the meal was German-inspired.

Once they'd eaten, he, Finley, and Jamie headed to one

of the private conference rooms to talk. Finley gave him a hard stare. "Jamie asked that I include you in this meeting, but I'm not entirely sure why. Can you give me a bit of background as to why you're here?"

For the first time in days, Tucker felt in his element. He smiled and relaxed. "I hear, Lord Finley," the man flinched, but Tucker was fine with that; this was an interview, and he'd wait for an invitation to drop the title, "you may be as good as me at IT security. I was hired straight out of college, though my love of the challenge started well before my years in academia. Within a year, I proved myself to the company and showed them why they should promote me to top-tier management. If they hadn't, I could've gotten a job in several other companies in Chicago, or really, any large city in the U.S. My knowledge and skill with IT security has yet to be foiled."

He turned from Finley to Jamie and smiled before continuing. "More than that, I've designed, built, and maintained computer systems several times in my life. In my current role as head of IT security, I am in a position where I interview, hire, and train new staff. I think, if you put all of that together, I can be helpful to you and Jamie."

As he spoke, Finley's face stayed hard and impassive. In the end, his eyes sparkled and he smiled. "Most of what I heard, besides my title—which you'll never use again outside of an official function—is that you want a throw-down, *Lord* Tucker."

Excitement bloomed in Tucker and he sat up taller. "Really? Are there two systems we can use? I am so hard-up for something fun to do. Sitting by the pool has been killing me."

Finley began to vibrate in his seat. "I can remove my computers from the system here. I've been wanting to check out the full spectrum of their current set-up. Why don't you take the day to do a full inventory and test of the computer room? You and Jamie can start compiling a list of what they have and need. Personally, I need to get to 'King' class," he groaned. "And tomorrow, after breakfast, we play."

Tucker spent the rest of the day in the basement. He wanted to throw out everything in the room. Even Jamie, who knew little about technology, agreed. "I didn't know monitors came this…deep."

"Yeah, they haven't been that inefficient in…wow. This is old." Tucker rubbed his temples. "I can't battle Finley on this. I'm going to grab my laptop. As old and out of date as it is, it's better than anything in this room." He'd left his fancy computer at home, but brought the laptop that fit in his backpack, he couldn't go completely without any of his toys. "It won't be enough to beat Finley, if my guess is correct, but this current system is atrocious. I'll get it hooked up and see what we have. Then we'll spend the afternoon restructuring and making lists. This will be expensive. We have to start over from scratch."

Jamie winked. "Don't worry, our budget's big!"

Once his laptop was integrated into the system, the security system felt like a chain-link fence around an amusement park, not an impenetrable wall. If there was a chance of slowing a hacker down for even a second, he'd have to rearrange things. It took a few hours, but by the time he was done, he'd used up a bit of the budget and fortified the firewall—well, created a small one, installed some software, and merged his own programming with industry standard to make it better. Some of what he created was illusion and trickery.

Spinning in his seat, he rubbed his temples, and spoke to Jamie in a tired voice. "Okay, new goal. If I can hold Finley off for over ten minutes, I get a prize. Every five minutes after that, the size of the prize increases. There was nothing there. It was worse than disgusting. I've created…well, something."

"And if I snatch your digital flag in under ten minutes?"

The man of the hour sauntered in and Tucker smiled at him with a shrug. "Since I believe a ten year old could, I guess it wouldn't be much of a surprise. Did you know there wasn't anything here?"

Finley dropped in a spinny chair and spun once in a full circle. "Wasn't? As in, there's something now?"

Jamie leaned against a table, her long legs crossed, a mug of tea cradled in her hands. "I approved a bit of expenditure for this silly game the two of you are playing."

Finley's face lit up. "Brilliant. I look forward to the battle. Did you set a prize?"

Tucker lifted an eyebrow. "I did. Once you get in, you can flash the lights in this room and stop the timer I have set up on that monitor." He pointed over his shoulder. "I have it rigged to show a visual representation of the challenge to anyone who wants to watch."

Finley stopped fidgeting. "You did all of that since we separated this morning?"

Jamie laughed. "Don't think too hard. I learned to just let it wash over me years ago. Tucker starts to explain what he considers an average amount of work…and, well, just let it go. It's because—"

Every muscle in Tucker's body tensed. Voice strained, he said, "Jamie." He didn't need her explaining anything more than he'd already shared. "It's nothing, really. We'll have our little face off tomorrow after breakfast. It'll be a hoot. I just hope I have the agility to hold you off for ten minutes, like I said."

Cold seeped into his bones and he no longer felt the thrill he'd had all day. He forced a smile at each of them. "If you don't mind, I think I'm going to take myself off to bed. Must be clear-headed for tomorrow's adventures."

He heard the knocking on his door, but ignored them, pretending to be asleep. He didn't want to talk to either Jamie or Emma. He'd acted a bit foolish, but he didn't want people knowing his past. It was embarrassing. He just wanted his life to have started at college. Emma knew more since she was part of it, practically his sister. Jamie knew because she was his best friend. To him, that was more than enough people who knew his origins.

He agonized, trying to forget that last conversation. Finley probably thought he was an idiot. Well, he'd prove it when the man left him in the dark, literally, in a few minutes at their challenge. Despite all Tucker's work, nothing he did would amount to a hill of beans. Their game would be a quick slaughter.

The next day after breakfast, Anastasia, Malcolm, Emma, and Adrian followed him and Jamie down to the basement. Finley headed up to his computers. Tucker yearned to see the man's computer set up, but figured that wasn't in the cards.

He'd brought down his headphones to drown out the talk of the people watching.

Once he'd gotten everything set up, he realized that he'd missed some of the spectators who'd ventured down for the spectacle; the Queen and her advisor, Sidney, had joined them as well. His show was streaming live for the entire royal entourage. Thankfully, he trained in front of crowds often enough he was used to being watched… though this was more pressure than usual.

Trying not to let that shake him, he faced Jamie. "If you could turn on the TV?"

"This will be like the smack-down sophomore year against the seniors. You'll leave him in the dust." She smiled

"You know you're talking about your boss."

She huffed a laugh before turning on the TV. He made sure that the first image matched what he'd set up.

"Eh, he doesn't know what he's gotten himself into fighting you. I'll always back my friend."

Tucker had created a visual of the palace with as much detail as he could. It wasn't much better than blocky, rough shapes, but with the time he had, he couldn't do more. There was a white wall around the palace with flames on top. He'd rendered a knight on a horse circling just inside the 'fire wall.' In the top right corner was a timer. Once Finley had beaten him, the time would stop.

He slid on his headphones and prepared to immerse himself in the code. Out loud he said, "Jamie, tell Finley we'll start in three, two, one." He clicked 'enter' on his keyboard. "Now." The last word was spoken almost in a whisper as he sank into his work.

His world became like playing cards, the system as it

should be. He flipped through each one, and they were each slightly different. He flipped faster and faster, checking for blips that would indicate a change from what he originally predicted. Some differences were expected—people working on computers in different areas of the palace. He searched for something truly different—something abnormal.

When he trained new people, he had each person design a mental landscape that made sense to them; it helped to follow the code better. The image of flipping through cards always resonated with him.

All his focus stayed on his laptop; old and slow, but better than anything in the palace's computer room. As he searched, he imagined his avatar prowling the grounds for the spectators to watch on the TV screen, searching, sniffing, the horse's hoof beating the ground in challenge.

Each of his cards were what he expected—until one of the images was too perfect. He honed in on it and began unwrapping it. It repaired itself almost as fast as he tore it apart. It wasn't correct, it wasn't what the wall was supposed to look like. Something was out of place.

He started tossing up pre-prepared obstacles to slow Finley down. Spheres that encompassed the area. He stepped out of the sphere and created a second, trying to find the man. He could feel him, but he couldn't see him. He circumnavigated the third sphere he put up, but he still couldn't find him. As soon as he felt Finley tear through the second sphere, he began repairing the escape route, fixing the hole he'd come through while trying to trap him. But his traps weren't strong enough.

He growled. This wasn't going well. He slid back into the palace and found Finley near the center. He put up a wall, his last offensive trap, and knew the seconds were burning up before his eventual failure. Knowing he had no other option, he followed the trail back and took images of the IP address, accessed Finley's camera and took a picture of him as well. He sent those to Finley's phone once he realized what the man wore. He didn't want to put them up on the screen for the whole Royal family to see.

Then the lights went out and he flopped back in his seat, defeated.

CHAPTER 11

The bell above the door jingled, and before Casimir could head out to greet the guest, Tucker's voice came through the open door. "It's just me. Should I come back?"

Casimir stopped halfway to the door. It had been several days since he'd seen the palace's envoy. He'd begun to wonder if Tucker had somehow gotten out of the chore. Then again, with this type of planning, daily updates really weren't needed. "Sure, come on back."

Tucker came through the opening dressed as immaculately as he had been the first time. He wore black trousers that hugged his body and a snug cerulean polo shirt, tucked in, with a matching belt. For a man who claimed to not know fashion, he certainly dressed well.

After his quick appraisal, he turned back to his work. "Do you want to get the summary over with now or at the end?"

Tucker stepped up next to Casimir, almost touching. His heat warmed Casimir's arm and sent a jolt of desire through him. "Either is fine, but I was wondering, my small notebook…it didn't make it back to the palace with me. I was hoping I left it in your car. Maybe when that biker cut you off. Did you find it after I left? If not, can we check? Otherwise I'll have to trouble you for something to write on and write with."

Casimir made a show of searching his workroom strewn with paper and pencils. "I don't know if I could *possibly* find anything else for you to write on or with if we can't find your notebook…but yes, let's go check the car."

Tucker chuckled. "Fair, though there were more than notes about your work in there and it *would* be nice to find."

They headed out to the car, but his notebook wasn't there. Back in the workroom Casimir found another small notebook he could live without—the cover was emblazoned with his own logo—and he gave it to Tucker. He also provided a pencil embossed with the Ixica Couture brand. It amused him that Tucker would now be writing in Casimir's own gallery merchandise.

Casimir quickly ran down everything he'd done over

the last few days, and his goals for the morning. Tucker had the far-off look Casimir associated with cataloging everything away for future study. It instilled confidence in him. He then gave a curt nod and smiled. Tucker's smile cheered Casimir. "Well, off to my corner…unless you'd rather I leave. I think the walk would be short."

Casimir shook his head and rolled his eyes. *These Americans and their hasty ways.* "I actually thought, if you could give me an hour, I would give you a better tour of the city. The idea you've been here as long as you have and no one's thought to show you the place is a travesty."

He was rewarded with one of Tucker's true smiles. It turned him from pretty to breathtaking. "I'd really like that. I've spent the last four days in the basement of the palace setting up their computers and then interviewing people for a job I want. The new staff will be excellent, once they've been trained to my standards. Being away for a few hours would probably be a smart choice…you know, before I turn into a troll."

"Oh! You got to do some of what you're good at; no wonder you seem lighter. Excellent. Okay, give me an hour to finish what I was doing, and we can be off."

It took closer to an hour and a half, but Tucker didn't seem to mind. He had been doing something in the notebook, closing it quickly as soon as Casimir walked up to him. Curiosity overtook him. "What were you doing?"

He snorted. "Doodling, like any good kid wasting time in class."

They returned to his car, but Casimir noticed the notebook and pencil were secured in the door's pocket. No leaving it behind this time. They drove around, and Casimir explained about the architecture and art. He loved the city and its rich history.

After a couple of hours, Casimir's stomach growled. "Hungry?"

Tucker, whose nose was practically glued to the window, turned to face him. "Oh, I could eat. Anything good around here?"

"One of my favorite Irish-themed pubs is down this street, they have a great fish and chips, if you're interested."

Tucker slumped back with a contented sounding sigh. "Sounds divine."

They parked and headed in, finding a table in the corner. The waitress came over and stuck out her hip. "The usual?"

"Make it two, and put it on my tab."

She returned shortly with two pints of beer. Tucker took a sip and groaned. "This will go to my head, so only one." He proceeded to drink down half the glass. "I know what I said, and I mean it, but I've been so stressed, and God this takes the edge off."

Casimir considered the stress of going on vacation with his best friends. "The last four days were stressful?"

"Yes, well, no." He closed his eyes and sighed. "I just… Jamie is never returning to Chicago, and Emma has so much more going on in Chicago. I had hoped…but then I didn't say anything to Finley because I'm a freaking idiot. Instead I just helped them hire other people who aren't half as good as me. Now I'll train them. And then I'll be sent back to Chicago…alone."

As Tucker drank the last of his beer, Casimir thought he followed Tucker's ramblings. He didn't want to leave, but he hadn't presented his case to stay. Maybe if he had, Finley would've hired him instead of one of the other new IT staff. "Why not ask Finley to hire you anyway? If you'll be training the others, you're obviously an asset."

He picked up his glass, then realized it was empty with a shrug. "I don't know. I don't advocate well for myself. My confidence comes in stages, and obviously I used it all up when I demanded my promotion a few years ago. I think I want this too much."

Casimir signaled for another beer. He knew what Tucker had said, and he could not drink it, but he seemed to still need to get more of the edge off. "Do you have a boyfriend or anything like that back home?"

He snorted, shaking his head. "I have my job. I sometimes feel like I'm married to it."

CHAPTER 12

Tucker heard the words come out of his mouth and frowned. "It isn't that bad. I do go out and have fun, I just…no, to answer your question, I don't have anyone back in Chicago. You? Are you in a relationship?"

He saw Casimir physically shutter at the word. "Do *not* say that word to me. I work with people wanting to get married…and divorced. Relationships are not all they're cracked up to be."

The waitress brought Tucker another beer and he knew he was already tipsy. He hadn't eaten enough, but at this point, he didn't care. He picked it up, saluted his handsome table-mate, and took a healthy swig. "You won't hear arguments from me, my friend."

His head began to buzz and he knew he was in trouble. As long as Casimir didn't ask any serious questions, everything would be okay. Casimir tilted his head. "I know why I don't like marriage. Why are you against it?"

Tucker shut his eyes and debated the beer he held. *Fuck it.* With a groan, he drank more. He'd stopped Jamie from possibly telling his story, and though he didn't like people knowing it, there was something about Casimir... or possibly it was the beer.

Taking another sip may stay his tongue. He lifted the glass and couldn't stop the memories, or his need to tell the beautiful man across from him about them. "I don't usually tell people this...but...I don't know." He bit his lip and couldn't stop himself. "Until I was thirteen, I lived with my parents. They fought every night, screaming loud enough I swear they kept half the neighborhood awake. I remember the night I told them I preferred boys to girls, my dad had been teasing me about some girl who'd just moved in down the street and how pretty she was. I'd had enough of his teasing."

His hands began to shake and he put down the beer after one more swig. All his memories of the people who birthed him were filled with hate and depression. "My dad said I had a choice; I could join this program the church put on to 'retrain the queer out of people' and find Jesus, or I could leave…no longer be part of the Larson family."

Casimir's brows twitched together and his eyes narrowed. "I thought your last name was Black."

Tucker huffed out a laugh before finishing his beer. "Oh, it is…now. When I packed a bag and headed for the door I was warned if I walked out I would never be welcome back again." His head hurt and the memories jabbed up to the top like painful stabs to his brain. "Emma's family took me in. Periodically they reached out to my parents to see if they'd reconsider. Eventually, they told Emma's mom if she didn't stop they'd take out a restraining order on her. That was after they learned Emma's sister was transgender. It was too much for them…all that *acceptance*." Tucker sneered out the last word like he imagined his parents would have done to Emma's mom.

A third beer appeared next to Tucker and he slowly shook his head. "You, sir, are going to get me throughly drunk." The beer had arrived with food, so he'd started in on that instead. Thinking about Emma's parents made him smile, but he wanted to get all the ugly out. "Needless to say, I haven't seen my parents since then, and though Emma's parents are lovely, as are Jamie's, the parents who raised me proved that aiming for a relationship isn't always what one should go for. Knowing who brought me into the world, I'm probably broken merchandise anyway." He gazed down at himself. "I'm not sure why anyone would even want me." He mumbled the last between bites of delectable fish.

CHAPTER 13

Casimir sipped his second beer and ate his lunch. His upbringing had been rough, but nothing like this. He could see why Tucker didn't share this story often. He was happy Tucker's friend and her family had taken him in at thirteen. Still, thirteen years with the parents he had would've left scars.

As he watched Tucker tuck into his food, and sip on his third pint of beer, he knew the man couldn't return to the palace; he was drunk. He'd finally fully relaxed and Casimir didn't think the people in the palace, save Emma and Princess Jamie, were ready to see him like this.

He could possibly contact one of the two women and get them to collect Tucker, but Casimir wasn't sure if that was what he wanted to do. It *had* been awhile, and despite what the man thought of himself, plenty of men would want him.

Tucker washed down a bite of food and gazed at Casimir. "You are so handsome, did you know that? What I couldn't do with someone like you for a night." He slowly lowered the mug then shook his head as if trying to decide if he'd really just said that aloud.

Casimir rubbed his chin, debating. "You wouldn't want to come back to my place for the evening, would you?"

Tucker's head shot up and he shook it as if trying to clear his mind. "I know I'm a wee bit drunk, and may be imagining things…I usually don't let myself get like this… but did you just invite me back to your place? Because if you did, that'd be really swell." His head lolled a bit to the side, but he spoke remarkably well for someone half-way through his third pint when he had been wary of his first.

Letting go of his mug, Tucker glared at it. "Can I get some water? I think I should try to clear my head. I'm not clever enough to spend more time with you at the moment."

As Casimir waved down the waitress, Tucker put some serious effort into finishing off his food. Once the plate was emptied, and he'd had a glass of water, he rubbed his temples and sighed. "Okay, I think I may be sobering up a bit. I'm starting to regret everything I told you, which means my inhibitions are returning. So…that's good."

Casimir raised a single eyebrow and smiled at him. "If your inhibitions are back, are you turning my invitation down?"

The look of horror that crossed his face was worth the question. "God, no, I've fantasized about that question since I studied every inch of your body when you walked in front of me for dinner that first night. Oh, crap, no filter. No more beer." He pushed the beer away as if it were filled with bugs.

Smiling mischievously, Casimir pushed the glass of beer back. "Oh, I don't know. You're kind of fun like this. Let's see what other questions I can think to ask. It's like a weird super power, isn't it?"

Eyes widening, Tucker slapped his hands over his mouth and shook his head.

Casimir stood and threw some bills on the table. "Well, come now, let's see how you look out of those clothes. I, too, have been wondering since that first night. You, with your impeccable style and clothing and the face of an angel who claims no fashion sense."

The drive back to his studio was quick. The tour had been over an hour, but they'd driven a circuitous route. Casimir led Tucker up to his private apartment and to the small bedroom. The room was big enough for a queen-sized bed and a dresser. Once inside, Casimir pulled the other man in for a quick kiss that turned deep and penetrating, curling Casimir's toes. Tucker's hands roamed over his back and butt, pulling out Casimir's shirt and finding skin to caress.

Casimir pulled back. "Last chance. You were pretty tipsy back at the restaurant. Is this what you want?"

Tucker looked back at him with a wide smile. "More than you know. Drunk, sober, yes, I want this." He reached around to the front of Casimir's pants and only struggled with his belt for a moment before getting the clasp undone and opening the button and zipper underneath. He gasped in what sounded like delight. *He must have discovered I don't wear underwear.*

Casimir's thoughts short-circuited as Tucker's warm hand grasped his cock and began stroking. His head fell back and he groaned as pleasure shot through him. Casimir shut his eyes, focusing on the man in front of him.

Having designed and dressed as many people as he had, Casimir expertly divested Tucker of his shirt and pants, belt and all. He pushed the man back for a moment. "Let's fully remove these before one of us falls—namely you, drunk boy. Then we can continue."

If Casimir were honest, he needed a second to collect himself. His body felt electrified from the kisses and touches. He worried he'd explode then and there if they *didn't* slow down. He watched as Tucker pulled off shoes and pants, careful not to fall over. Step by step revealing a perfectly sculpted body with patches of hair in all the right places.

He wanted pictures he could refer to every time he was alone and touching himself. Such a perfect body deserved celebration. Fully naked, Tucker turned to him and smiled. "What, am I the only one getting naked?"

Casimir felt the heat rise to his cheeks, and wondered when the last time he blushed was. Tucker landed on the end of the bed and watched him, stroking himself in obvious enjoyment. "You are one of the sexiest men I've ever seen, designer man. Did you know that? So damn hot."

Quickly stripping off his clothes, Casimir climbed into the bed, and Tucker followed. Tucker slid his hand behind Casimir's head and leaned down for a kiss. His hand roamed down Casmir's chest, pinching his nipple along the way. Casimir gasped into his mouth, nibbling on his lower lip in return.

Tucker shifted to his side, letting his mouth fall to Casimir's ear. "I want to taste you…until you scream."

Casimir groaned, his body tightening in response as Tucker lifted to hands and knees and began licking and kissing down his body. When he got to Casimir's nipples he captured each one in his teeth and gave a small tug. He continued lower, and as he reached Casimir's cock, his hand dipped between his legs, grasping his balls as his mouth sucked in his length.

With a jerk, every nerve in Casimir's body lit up. Lightning shot out from his groin to the rest of his body, and heat gathered, ready to overtake him. His whole being became Tucker and his hands and mouth as they sucked him in, tight and hot.

The man's mouth licked and played, tasting him. Lowering down with a tight suction caused a wave of chills. Casimir arched up needing more. Tucker pulled up, tongue lapping on his throbbing cock. Fingers playing with his balls, the other hand squeezing the end of his member, Casimir's body became nothing but the heat and pleasure growing within him.

He felt Tucker's mouth suck and he thought he'd pass out as the sensations intensified, his body trembling through the orgasm. The world fractured around him as he bucked up again and yelled out the man's name, his seed filling Tucker's mouth.

CHAPTER 14

Tucker woke up, his legs intertwined with Casimir's. Everything hurt. His head pounded, he felt nauseous, and his memory of the night before made him giddy. They'd played for hours. He couldn't remember when a bout of sexcapades had been so fun.

If he were to be honest, it had been too good. He probably shouldn't have spent the night with the designer, but as much as he'd fantasized about the man, there was no way he'd have said no. Not with Casimir's interest. He'd never find another person who made his body sing like that.

He closed his eyes and took one more moment to

appreciate the sensation of Casimir beside him, naked and perfect, then he shifted position. Casimir stretched, rolled over, and kissed him. "Hi, beautiful. How is your head this morning?"

Tucker chuckled, then groaned as the pounding intensified in his head. "When did you install a full band with drummers in my head? I feel like I got hit by a truck. *Did* I get hit by a truck?"

Casimir moved over him and all Tucker's muscles tightened, igniting. The pain in his head doubled as he lifted his body to maximize contact. He moaned, unable to determine what he wanted. He caught Casimir's mouth with his own, exploring the designer's taste, wrapping his leg around him, but then someone jammed a piston through his temple.

He fell back, panting for air. "God above, I want this, but I think I'm dying. My head, I…I can't believe I'm saying this…but…I can't. I have to go." He closed his eyes and draped his arm across his eyes. Sadness at the thought of leaving fought with the hangover he battled, but he wouldn't enjoy staying and he wanted to enjoy his time in Casimir's bed.

Casimir's warm hand cupped his cheek. "I'll drive you."

Tucker shook his head and rolled from the bed. Having Casimir touch him was too much. It ignited his desire, and all the feelings made his head pound harder. "I'll walk."

"That's crazy; it's over three kilometers."

He squeezed his eyes shut and rubbed his forehead. "You Europeans and your forcing me to think…ah…that's about two miles. That's my walk to work most mornings." He took a few breaths to help his throbbing head. "It would be good for me to get fresh air."

It only took a few minutes to find his clothes and slip them on. He made it to the stairs and through the shop to the front door. He stopped and stared. If he left the shop, it would be unlocked. He didn't see anyone out the windows, but if Casimir felt half as bad as him, then he wasn't ready for customers, and none of his workers were in yet.

From behind him he heard, "Don't worry, I'll lock it up behind you…unless you've changed your mind."

Not able to resist Casimir, he went up to him and gave him one more kiss before leaving the shop.

The morning was cool, and though his head hurt, moving felt good. He knew he needed something in his belly. He stopped at a coffee shop for some caffeine. The battle for supremacy between the grunge band playing in his head and the mostly black coffee was fierce, and he was glad the palace was so obvious ahead of him during his walk.

By the time he arrived at the palace he only felt like basic hell. A few staff were about, and he smiled at them as he trudged up the stairs to his room. Once there, he showered and changed into jeans and a t-shirt. He slowly made his way back down to the family dining room to grab breakfast. The only people there were Emma and Prince Adrian…flirting. *Gah, too much this early in the morning with a pounding headache. I just can't!*

He spun on his heel to escape and sought out a servant. Though still uncomfortable with servants and asking others to do things for him, the thought of socializing was worse. His pain and the trembling in his body decided his next actions. He requested a breakfast sandwich and large coffee be brought down to the computer room, then headed there himself.

The new computers hadn't yet arrived, but two of the three new staff reviewed the recording of his competition with Finley, which had lasted thirteen minutes…lucky him. He'd joked with Jamie about a prize for anything over ten minutes and he still hadn't decided on what he'd get.

As he walked in, the staff began to bombard him with questions. With an effort of will, he shifted to a headspace that wasn't pounding with a hangover. *Thank god I can do this in my sleep, or halfway in a coma!* The next few hours were lost in IT security training, review, and teaching.

CHAPTER 15

Casimir gazed at his boards without seeing them. His mind kept sliding back to the previous day and night, the bed play, and waking up with Tucker entwined with him. He groaned. At first he thought the man was just pretty, but he proved he was more: smart, funny, and kind. Casimir enjoyed their time together. There weren't a lot of people he liked to spend time with.

Get your mind on your work, Casimir, he was a fun romp. Nothing more. What is it about the man that's gotten under your skin?

He reached down to drag the nearest board closer. He

thought about the shirt Tucker had worn the day before and smiled. A bit of an accent color would do nicely. He let his mind wander, imagining the event, the people, their outfits, and the color story he wanted to create. Casimir finally sank into his work and spent the next hour lost in the future ceremony.

A buzz from his pocket pulled him out. He quickly checked the display and saw a message from Malcolm. Queen would like a personal update. Current summaries great, but visuals would be better. 11am? Then lunch?

Outside of having an actual emergency, there was only one answer to give to this text. He sent off a quick affirmative. Casimir called Tabatha to gather all his work for the wedding and coronation then headed up to his apartment to look over his outfit.

He wore gray slacks with a fitted forest green sweater. He searched his closet and found a gray jacket that buttoned at his neck with a scoop hem that went just past his knees. It was a shade darker than his pants and played off the green well enough. In his bathroom he double-checked his hair then stepped back, wondering who he was primping himself for. He hadn't put this much care into his outfits any other time he went to the palace.

Will Tucker even be at the meeting?

He stepped from his apartment and grumbled at his

own silliness, heading back down to find two portfolios and a small notebook stacked on the table. Tabatha saw him coming and waggled her brows at him. "Looking good. I wasn't sure where you wanted this. I assume with the coronation stuff?"

Casimir held out his hand and she handed over the small notebook. It wasn't his. He flipped through the pages and froze. It was Tucker's notebook from his initial visit. The first pages were filled with his notes—in shorthand, of all things. At least, he assumed that was what the weird notations on the pages were. Tucker had spent a few more pages writing a more detailed set of notes. They were still not complete, but interesting enough. Good details, for someone not qualified.

As Casimir flipped further through the book, his mouth dropped open. He arrived at what Tucker referred to as his 'doodles.' There were images of him in different stages of work. Some were mere sketches, but one was detailed enough, the image could step off the page, and Tucker had made him look beautiful.

Is this how he sees me? I know I put on a good front, but this is stunning.

Gazing at the image, Casimir's breath stuttered.

Turning the page again he saw a rendition of a crown from several angles. It held features of the current King's crown, but was subtly different. The following page had a scepter with a stylized top.

Casimir looked up at Tabatha. "Where did you find this?"

"It was in your car, on the floor. I just assumed it was yours, sir. The last few pages look like they belong with the coronation…was I wrong?"

Still a bit stunned, he shook his head. "Can you make a copy of the crown and staff and blow them up without losing any of the detail? Maybe the one of me in detail as well?"

She gave him a knowing smile before running off to do his bidding. Once he had everything packed, he headed to his car and made it to the palace with a couple of minutes to spare.

One of the palace staff led him up to a conference room. When he entered he found the Queen with her advisor, Sidney, as well as Malcolm, and Finley. Disappointment filled him when he realized Tucker wasn't there. The emotion shocked him. He headed for the far side of the table, and carefully set down his items. "Where is my liaison? I thought he would be here, since he's been so studious during his visits to the shop."

The Queen raised a brow. "His reports are rather thorough, but he didn't return to the palace last night until this morning." Her face remained impassive. "There are some bets as to where he may have gone last night. However, if you'd like, we'll send someone to find him."

Before he could answer, she signaled one of the servants who headed out the door. A second servant asked Casimir what he wanted to eat and a moment later he had a small cucumber sandwich and a cup of tea.

It didn't take long for Tucker to arrive. When he entered the room, wearing a pair of dark-wash jeans and a red t-shirt with the words, 'Love is Love' on it, he saw who was in the room, quickly looked down at his outfit, and froze, turning as red as his shirt. After taking a deep breath, he squared his shoulders, stood a bit taller, and nodded. "You called for me?" His face traveled over everyone in the room as if trying to figure out who requested him.

When his eyes landed on the Queen, she gave a slight bow. "We did, dear. Casimir is giving an in-person summary of what you've been writing up. What you're doing is perfect, but I wanted to see with my own eyes the designs and color you so vividly describe. I hope you weren't too busy."

After a moment of awkward silence, he tilted his head in a small bow and said, "Thank you, your Majesty, and no. I was working on showing the new-hires in the basement how I'd set up the TV you all watched when I'd gone up against Finley, er, Lord Finley…and failed miserably." He bowed his head again and went to sit at the end of the table furthest from the group.

Casimir glanced at Finley and Malcolm. The former was watching Tucker with narrowed eyes and a slight smile.

Once Tucker sat, a servant immediately moved to offer

him some food and drink.

Casimir decided it was time to pull out his boards and begin his presentations. He started with the wedding. He was mostly done with that event. It was just around the corner. Once he'd finished presenting his plan, he moved on to the coronation. No one but Tucker had seen any of this material. With a wink and a smile, he slowed down his presentation, allowing everyone to take in each of his ideas.

At the end, he pulled out Tucker's drawings. "As you know, this will be the first time the country of Ixica will be ruled by two Kings instead of a King and a Queen. Because of this, designing a new crown may not be a bad idea. While working with me in my studio, Lord Tucker created this idea for a new King's crown."

Tucker jerked at being called out. Everyone in the room appeared to be in a tennis match, since Tucker sat on the other side of the room from Casimir, looking first at his drawing, then at him, and then back to the drawing. The second perusal was much more intense, really trying to get a feel for what he'd created.

After a few minutes Casimir continued. "To go along with the crown, our newest Lord also designed a scepter." He put the second image up.

After everyone studied the second image in silence, the Queen asked, "Can they be made in time?"

Casimir nodded. "I believe they can. I just need your

approval of the design and I'll start getting estimates for manufacturing."

Malcolm's laugh echoed through the room. "If that isn't just brilliant. I had no idea we were sending you someone with skills beyond an amateur's. And why hadn't we thought of this?"

Sidney, who normally stayed silent in front of Casimir, turned to Tucker. "Lord Tucker, I'd personally like to shake your hand after this meeting. These designs are stunning."

It impressed Casimir how Tucker controlled the emotions that must be flowing through his body. He could see Tucker's hand tremble, but beyond that, the man sat tall and proud.

"Absolutely, Advisor Sidney, and thank you for the compliment."

CHAPTER 16

It took another quarter-hour for the meeting to finally end. Both the Queen and Malcolm had questions and suggestions. The rest of the group around the table sat, seeming to try to pretend interest. Tucker took some notes; this way he forced himself to stay focused. His mind still reeled that Casimir had taken his notebook, looked through it, and used his doodles in the presentation.

He tried not to think about the other drawing he'd made. *What did he think about them? Was he offended? Maybe he didn't notice them…I should be so lucky.*

When everyone was satisfied, Sidney came over to shake

his hand as he'd threatened, and then everyone finally left. Tucker didn't know where to go, so he just put his head down on his crossed arms and waited for the room to empty.

A warm hand began to rub his back, letting him know his desire for solitude wasn't coming any time soon, though it did feel really good. With a sigh, he lifted his head, made sure it was Casimir. After assuring himself they were alone, he smiled at the designer, who leaned in for a kiss.

A small sound of contentment escaped Tucker, before he realized this had to stop. He was losing himself, and that would be a problem. He pulled back and licked his lips, savoring the flavor of the man next to him. "You had my notebook all along?" His voice came out sounding tired more than angry or accusatory.

Casimir laughed. "My assistant did. She found it in my car and assumed it was mine…nice doodles, by the way. You have some real talent…you're an artist." He said it as if it were a statement of fact.

Tucker warmed at the complement before he rubbed his face. "My art lies within the belly of a computer." He realized just how close Casimir sat to him. Their faces practically touched. He reached up and cupped the man's cheek. "I'm sorry, I can't do this again. You're too pretty, you can't also be nice…not if you're the average one night stand. You know, the 'love 'em and leave 'em' type. You have to follow through with the 'leave 'em' part of that so I can go lick my wounds. I'm good at that last part."

Casimir's face tightened under his hand and his eyes narrowed. "I told you up front who I was; you can't be angry with me."

Tucker shook his head. "I'm not. You did tell me, and I'm not blaming you. I'm just asking that you follow through with being the person you said you were. It hurts. It'll hurt no matter what, but the more exposure I have to you, the nicer you are, the more I feel my insides…no, I'm not going to tell you; it isn't fair. Thank you for an amazing night."

Casimir's hand came up to cup Tucker's cheek so that the two mirrored each other. "What about the fact that you're my liaison? And that in a couple of days you'll be sitting in my shop working with me?"

Tucker laughed a humorless laugh and rolled his eyes. "Let me worry about that. I mean, I'll be asking for that job to work here permanently, and like everything else, it'll probably be denied. I'll heal; it's what I do. I'll get kicked to the curb, fly back to Chicago, and I'll have my job back there waiting for me with open arms. It will be my whole life again."

Casimir's head tilted. "But more so because at least one of your friends will be staying here."

He shrugged. "I figured out how to survive before, I'll do it again."

With a sadness behind his gaze, Casimir stared deep into Tucker's eyes. Finally, he nodded before pulling back, collecting his stuff, and heading for the door. Tucker sat like a statue as he listened to the footsteps retreat down the hallway.

He may have stayed there for a lot longer, but his stomach began yelling at him. He started to head to the dining room, but realized he wasn't in the mood to be around other people. Heading into the kitchen, he asked if he could sit at the small table in there. No one seemed to mind, and he relaxed in blissful solitude. The buzz of the people working around him became white noise.

When he was almost done with a meat pie, Emma's head popped around the corner. "There you are! We've been looking everywhere for you." She came in and plopped down next to him. Coming in behind her, Adrian sat at the table as well. The two beamed at him.

Despite his private moment being disturbed, Tucker was thrilled to see his best friend in all her exuberance. Plates of food were brought for each of them as well as glasses of wine. Tucker sipped at his water. "To what do I owe the pleasure of your company?"

Emma blushed. "Okay, I have some news and we were debating how to tell people. I knew I had to tell you first, even before I called home to tell Mom and Dad and Jojo."

Tucker's brow rose. He had a sinking feeling he knew exactly what was coming next, but wasn't going to try to predict and ruin her moment.

She started to bounce. "Okay, okay, okay, here it is.

Adrian asked me to marry him and I said yes." Her voice rose to a squeal. "We're getting married!"

She launched herself at him and he wrapped his arms around her in a hug that let her know how happy he was for her. She was the only family he really had and her happiness meant everything to him. Squeezing her, he smiled at Adrian. "I don't know how much she's told you about me—and of course she's welcome to tell you what she wants—but she's my sister, you know. I'm happy for you both. Be good to her. She deserves the stars and the moon and so much more. She saved me when I was young, and I hope you know what a treasure she is."

He knew he babbled by the end, tears flowing from his eyes. But it hit him: he was losing his last connection from home. When he returned to Chicago, everyone he loved would be staying in Ixica.

CHAPTER 17

Casimir woke and lay in bed, relaxing. It was the morning of the wedding and his mind was busy, cataloging all the things he would need to do before the big event. He realized he'd see Tucker, whom he hadn't seen in person since the presentation for the Queen, and he wasn't sure if he was excited or apprehensive. No one else had come as liaison, so he figured everyone was happy with what he'd put together. He had been in and out of the palace in the intervening time to set things up, but hadn't seen Tucker.

He sat up, rubbing his head. *Why am I thinking of that damn man? It's been days. The point of the romp was to get him out of my system, not make me think of him more.*

Despite his decision that it would remain a one night stand, he'd hoped for a couple of nights. When Tucker had turned him down, it had shocked him. In all his dalliances, he'd always been the one to walk away; it hurt and distracted him to be on the other side. *Focus, you fool. He's one man, not worth all this. Sexy, yes, smart, absolutely, good in bed…God above, stop thinking about that, you're on a schedule…*

He forced his mind to think about what he had to do. Standing up, his gaze landed on the small, framed picture of himself he'd copied from Tucker's notebook. With a groan he tipped it face down and headed to the shower. He could take care of himself there and then get dressed. If he happened to think of Tucker and his night playing with him while touching himself, no one but him would know.

From his closet, he selected a light gray suit with a plum shirt and matching tie. Once he was sure he was picture perfect, he gathered anything he might need for the day—a travel sewing kit, extra fabric, snacks, an emergency kit created from years of attending events—and he was off to the palace. Everything else had been shipped over already.

The streets were quiet this early in the morning. Casimir watched the few early risers sitting behind the picture windows of the coffee shop as he drove by. He wondered if anyone would be up at the palace, or if he'd be alone in the ballroom, preparing the dream wedding of a man who'd quickly become a close friend of his. Even if no one else was up, he wanted to ensure Malcolm's and Finley's wedding was perfect.

After he parked, he waved off the servant and navigated the halls to the large ballroom in the back of the palace where the wedding would take place. As he neared the back hallway, sounds echoed down the corridor. He peeked in the room and saw Tucker holding a notebook directing a dozen staff members, his rich voice issuing orders.

Leaning against the doorframe, Casimir admired Tucker from afar. He was absolutely stunning, imposing even, as he took command. From his stories of back home, Casimir knew he was a leader, but he'd never seen him in action, and Casimir's desire to run up to him and strip his clothes off was almost overwhelming.

The staff looked to Tucker for direction with respect. His instructions were clear and unwavering. He wanted things done quickly and precisely. When he saw something clumsily completed, he redirected the person, complimenting the bits done well, and showing him or her exactly how to do the job properly.

Eventually, Tucker turned to survey the full room and he spotted Casimir. His eyes widened and his shoulders slumped. After a slight nod, he spun back to the group and gave a few more directions, then retreated to the far side of the room.

The spot behind Casimir's breastbone ached. He wasn't sure why, and he didn't know what to do about it, but seeing Tucker walk away from him made his body tingle with pain. Part of him wanted to call after the man, but his impulse to do so confused him. He shook his head, befuddled. None of this made any sense to him.

A hand landed on his shoulder from behind. Shocked, his heart skipped a beat, and his head snapped back. "If it weren't your wedding…" He gulped in some air. "You scared the living daylights out of me, Malcolm."

Malcolm gave him a goofy half-smile. "You should go after him."

Casimir scratched his chin. "Tucker? Why?"

With a shake of his head, Malcolm shrugged. "Really? That's how you're going to play this?"

"I don't run after men, Malcolm. They seek me out."

A single royal brow lifted. "It's obvious something happened there. There is hurt between you two. Go fix it before you ruin my wedding."

Snarling, Casimir glared at his friend before stomping off in the direction he saw Tucker disappear.

There weren't many places the man could've gone on this floor, and he didn't want to search if he didn't have to. He started in the pool area and found him sitting at a table near the kitchenette. What luck.

Before stepping out onto the pool deck, Casimir took a

moment to center himself, watching Tucker as he sat, elbows on knees, head in hand. He looked miserable. Casimir slipped through the silent door and made his way to the table, and sat in the chair next to Tucker. "How're you doing?"

He didn't move. If he hadn't spoken, Casimir wouldn't have known he noticed his presence at all. "I'm heading back to Chicago in a couple of days…probably alone. Everyone I care about, love, and who cares for me, will be staying here. I'll be alone once I leave here. How do you think I'm doing?"

Casimir could feel the pain emanating for him. "What about Emma…Lady Emma?"

Tucker's fingers started to massage his head. "Emma is fine, no titles between us…please. It all makes my head hurt worse. She's staying…she won't be returning with me."

"Can you stay?"

"I asked. I had a meeting with Finley and Adrian and presented why I would be a good addition to the palace staff. I've been working with the new hires, training them. I know that's counter-intuitive; I just can't help myself. But anyway, they said they'd discuss it with the Queen and Sidney. Bringing me in involves a bunch more paperwork."

Casimir leaned back, a bad feeling growing in his gut. "How long ago?"

With a sigh, Tucker finally sat back and met Casimir's gaze. "Too long. I can read between the lines. It shouldn't have taken more than a day or two to decide if I was worth hiring." He shrugged. "So, after the wedding I'll be shipped back home." His eyes grew misty, though he set his jaw as if fighting it.

Casimir tilted his head and wondered if the Royal family knew how much they were tearing their guest apart. He doubted it; his guess was Tucker hid all of this from everyone. For some reason, even after everything, Tucker was opening up to him. The Royal family had to know an answer; even an answer of 'no' would be better than leading Tucker on. And the idea they were using him to train their IT staff without compensation and seemingly not having any qualms about that bothered Casimir. "For my part, I'm sorry."

He went to reach out and place a hand on Tucker's leg, but the man moved away. "Please don't. 'Sorry' implies you'd have done something different. You wouldn't, and you aren't."

Casimir licked his lips. "I would like to…I don't know. I would like more time with you."

"No." Tucker's head moved from side to side as he spoke. "I care more for my heart than to do that to myself. I could easily fall in love with you. Just…God, Casimir, just be mean. If you can't do that, continue to ignore me. I'll become hardened and jaded…eventually."

A punch to the gut would hurt less. When he spoke, he barely recognized his own voice. "I don't want you to become hardened or jaded. Your family didn't do it to you…I can't be that instrument."

Tucker looked at him with desperation in his eyes. "We can't both be happy."

It was too much. Casimir leaned forward, taking Tucker's chin in his hand, and kissed him. It felt like coming home. Something that had been hurting inside began to heal. He pulled back and licked his lips again, savoring the flavor. "I want both of us to be happy. Listen, your time here is limited. How about we go all in until they, as you implied, kick you to the curb? Not a one night stand, but you and me just doing our thing. I can't get you out of my mind, and I'd like to spend more time with you. Maybe you'll decide you hate me and that hurt in your eyes will go away." He traced the side of Tucker's face with his fingers. "But I can't seem to drag myself away from you."

Casimir was shocked at his words and how real they were. He wanted…needed more time with Tucker. *I crave him more than I've craved anything before.*

Tucker closed his eyes, shivering as Casimir rested his hand against the side of his face. His hands trembled as he slid them from his legs over to Casimir's. "I know I'm going to regret this…I'll be a puddle of pain and sorrow on the plane home, but leaving will tear me apart in so many other ways as well, what's one more." His eyes opened, and their gray depths seemed to sink into Casimir. "Let's do this."

A knot loosened in Casimir's chest and he breathed

freely for the first time in days. He thought all his tension had been about the wedding, but he'd been wrong.

He leaned in for a soft, sweet kiss. Tucker's hands rubbed up to Casimir's hips and he sighed.

Once the kiss ended, Casimir asked, "Will you come home with me tonight after the wedding?"

Tucker's only answer was a nod and a small smile.

CHAPTER 18

Tucker woke up to someone fondling his balls. He was either in an excellent dream, or—oh, God—he arched as his whole body tensed. He opened his mouth to get more air, unable to think or breathe, and a tongue invaded, searching, seeking, seducing.

He groaned as he wrapped his leg around Casimir's, kissing back. The man's hand moved faster and he bit down on Tucker's lower lip, scraping his teeth almost painfully away. He kissed his way to Tucker's ear, repeating the nip, before his tongue delved in, investigating. "I want you to come for me, Tucker. Be a good plaything, and scream for me."

The words reverberated through his head, and small pants and grunts were his only response. He couldn't find words. He began to buck up, his body's motions separate from any thought he may have had.

Heat built from his ear to his groin where Casimir's tongue and teeth played havoc with him. Then the man squeezed hard, his hand moved up and down his cock, and he said, "Come for me." It was too much. Tucker's body bowed. Hot seed spilled from him, landing on his stomach, as the waves of orgasm took him.

"Hmm," Casimir hummed in his ear. "Now it's my turn. On your side."

Tucker still shook with the tremors of his orgasm, but he rolled to his side. He felt the lube before Casimir pushed into him from behind. His body, still over sensitized, shivered as Casimir's body met his. He pushed back, loving the feel of the other man.

Casimir set a rhythm and Tucker lost all sense of anything as the pleasure built in him again. Warm hands on his hips as Casimir's thick, hot cock slid in and out of him. He lowered his hand to his own dick, his movements more jerky than smooth as sensations overcame him. His mind fractured as Casimir yelled out behind him with his release, the two of them panting and spent.

He lay curled up on his side as waves of ecstasy slowly dissipated. Casimir pulled him in so Tucker's head rested on his chest, stroking his back. Tucker wanted to purr in contentment. After a few minutes, Casimir got up and moved to the bathroom. Once he heard the shower, he decided that sounded like a good idea.

In the shower, he grabbed the soap and helped Casimir to clean himself off. Kissing down his chest, following the line of soapy bubbles after they washed away, he lowered himself to his knees to double check his cleaning.

He cupped Casimir's balls and thick cock as Casimir leaned against the wall of the small shower, a whimper escaping him. Tucker leaned closer as the slower water beat down on his head. He slid the pulsating member into his mouth, clasping the base with his hand, reveling in the feel of the hot, pulsating cock sliding into his mouth.

He groaned as it filled his mouth, the salty pre-cum flavoring his tongue. One hand played with the balls while the other squeezed the base of Casimir's cock. He rocked back and forth, pumping the cock in his mouth, his body hardening as it heated. One of Casimir's hands curled in Tucker's hair, tugging enough to make him moan.

His hands tightened on Casimir and the man bucked, forcing himself deeper down Tucker's throat. Eyes watering, he continued suck, the motion causing his own body to tighten further. Slipping his hand back, he slid a finger into Casimir's ass. Casimir jerked and his moans turned into a shout of pleasure as he orgasmed into Tucker's mouth.

As the cock in Tucker's mouth spasmed, the body in his hands tightened and released, and he broke, too. The power of bringing this man to this point was a powerful aphrodisiac. Hearing his name on Casimir's lips brought him to climax.

Once his own orgasm was done, he rested his head on Casimir's lower abdomen and rested as his body came down from its own high. After a few minutes, Casimir slid his hands under Tucker's arms to help him up, pulling him into an embrace, and kissing him deeply.

Finally clean, they both dried off and Tucker checked the time. He'd hidden out in Casimir's flat for two days, ignoring his phone and the outside world. "I think I should head back to the palace and see how things are going."

Casimir looked him up and down. "I don't know. You haven't had clothes on for two days, why start now?"

A smile broke out over Tucker's face. "Well, I *could* walk back naked, but I'm guessing that would be frowned on by the local authorities. I mean, I don't know all the laws around here…"

Digging fingers into his hips, Casimir slid their bodies together, lining their mouths up. "You are not walking, my lovely man, and you are not showing off your naked beauty for everyone else to see. I'm learning I don't want to share you…at least, not right now. I haven't tried everything out I want to try. You're like a new toy I'm thoroughly addicted to."

They were so close to kissing, but not quite there. "Fine, clothes first, *then* back to the palace." Not able to resist, Tucker played his hands up the man's silky smooth back, pulling him in for a deep, time-stopping kiss.

It took a bit longer to get to the palace, but he finally made it. They'd woken up early, and skipped food, but Tucker was still surprised when he walked into the family dining room for breakfast and found everyone there. He froze in the entry with all eyes on him.

Emma's and Jamie's faces lit up with knowing smiles. As for the others, he didn't want to know their reaction; his eyes remained on his friends. One of Emma's brows lifted. "So, you decided to join us for a meal? We thought you'd gotten lost after the wedding. No one's heard from you for days. Wanna fill us in?"

He slowly made his way to the empty seat between Adrian and Jamie. A plate of bacon and eggs with toast was put in front of him, and his stomach growled. Everyone was still gaping at him. "Um, I didn't think I'd be missed. I just…I'm fine, thanks for asking."

Jamie punched his shoulder. "Where the hell have you been, Tucker?"

Malcolm, sitting across from him, started to laugh. "You never checked your phone, did you? Two days with Casimir, and you never even thought to tell anyone."

Tucker's mouth dropped open. "How did you know?"

"Besides not being blind? He's also been out of contact for two days. It isn't hard to put one and one together. And, well, you just confirmed it."

With a groan, Tucker dropped his head into his hand. "I'm an idiot."

Obviously not trying to help, Malcolm said with a laugh, "Lack of sleep will do that to a person."

Tucker decided if he started eating his breakfast and drinking his coffee, maybe, just maybe, everyone in the room would ignore him. It wasn't the best plan, but it was the best he had. The coffee was ambrosia, and he had a few mugs before he felt like he could think.

Just when he thought he could follow the conversation, Finley stumbled in looking bleary. He sat by Malcolm, eyes wild-looking but focused only on his new husband. "Malcolm, I think I know why your dad was murdered."

Everyone in the room stopped what they were doing to stare at him. He picked up the coffee a servant had handed him and gulped it down. He seemed to realize he had a plate of food in front of him and quickly put everything on the bread to make a sandwich. "Can we go to a conference room, or somewhere private? This is…I don't want everyone to hear this."

Tucker watched as everyone stood. He leaned back, shocked at hearing about murder warring with his returning feelings of uselessness.

I wonder how long until they send me away. They don't

need to be hosting an American if whatever this is has Finley this out of sorts.

When everyone had filed out, he shut his eyes and debated what to do. He could go pack. There really wasn't much else to do in Ixica or any reason to delay his return to Chicago. He wasn't sure why he had, though the last few days had been fun. He wiped his face and stood.

Just as he turned to the door, Finley appeared. "Are you coming? I may need your help on this one."

He stood dumbfounded for a second before following the tall man to the room where everyone else had taken seats.

Finley paced the room. "I have been slowly checking over the old security of the palace. I know that Tucker has been doing it as well, as has the new staff. There was a wall that kept bugging me."

Tucker raised a brow. "The one on the south side of the pool? With the one off-colored brick?"

Finley froze and stared at him for a few seconds before giving a single nod. "Right, yes, that one. Behind that bit of code, I found a bunch of documentation that had gone back maybe a year. I copied to an external drive. I've since moved it to this drive. It is a series of emails and files from someone who was blackmailing the old King." Finley wiped his hands on his pants. "Here's the thing, I don't know how to say this…we need to verify it without raising suspicion…but, he claims to have proof that only Adrian is the King's son."

There was a beat of silence before the room erupted into chaos.

Finally the Queen stood up, her voice ringing out. "Silence!"

With the power only a Queen or a mother can wield, the room instantly went quiet. She stood gazing into the faces of the people sitting around the table. "When the King and I first married, we didn't think we could have children. In a very quiet ceremony, we adopted Anastasia and then Malcolm. You two are truly brother and sister. You two are your uncle's children. As you know, he was exiled after your grandparents' death. We know he wasn't responsible for their death, but a group got it in their head it was him. He never wanted to be King, so he left. Your father was young so Sidney agreed to stay and help us out."

She sat and picked up her tea, then gazed at Anastasia and Malcolm. "Your biological mother found herself pregnant twice. She didn't survive the second birth; it was nothing you did Malcolm, it was just complications. Well, your father contacted us and said he couldn't raise you two, he was heart-sick and having a baby nearly a year old and a newborn was beyond him. He couldn't give you two the love you deserved. We worried we couldn't have kids and decided then and there we had enough love. I'd been out of the country for most of the time, training to be Queen, so no one in Ixica had seen me. When we came back, no one questioned that you two were ours. A couple of years later, Adrian came along."

Anastasia shook her head. "Why haven't any of you ever told us?"

"Because, child, there was nothing to tell. You are my oldest child. Malcolm is my second oldest. Your father and I loved all three of you equally. Your uncle asked that he be left in the picture as only your uncle. He didn't want his exile to mess up your futures."

Shocked, Tucker looked around the room. Everyone's eyes were wide, mouths gaping. Apparently, he wasn't the only one completely gobsmacked by the news.

Malcolm's face got hard as stone. "We need someone to go after that person. He means to expose all of this. I do not want Father's or Mother's name sullied for adopting the children of a presumed traitor. Our father was a good man who did good things for this country."

Finley nodded. "I laid a trap when I left the code spot. If the person returns we can follow him or her back as well as get an image. I stole a bit of trickery that Tucker pulled on me during our chase."

Anastasia shook her head. "But how did this all lead to my father's death?"

Finley's shoulders dropped. "Right. The last message was an agreement to meet. It was set to happen shortly before the accident. Your father died in a car crash; his car went off a cliff. My guess is, after they met and spoke, your father refused the terms and the culprit messed with the electronics of his car. We'll need to double check the house and computer…once we find the bloody place, but there's bound to be more clues."

Adrian and Finley turned to Tucker and he felt his body both tingle and go numb. He'd just been thinking about packing to go home, and now the Royal family had a look. He felt like prey in someone's sights, and he wasn't sure if that was a good thing or bad.

Finley spoke first. "We need someone who we can trust to watch for this person and possibly go after him or her. Not only trust digitally, but when we find the person, to go clean up the system. Someone technologically savvy we can trust as well. Tucker, you are not only trustworthy, you're good at what you do."

"But when the person is found, I don't have a car to go anywhere, nor can I find my way around. And since this person found out about the King, they could figure out who in the palace is building up the fire wall and digital protections. If they are clever, will they go after people…I…um…care for? I would assume they're watching the palace and have figured out who we all are." He flinched at his own words. He didn't like the idea that he had any attachments.

Adrian's face scrunched up. "That's probably not an issue, but we could ask Casimir to move into the palace until this all blows over."

Tucker felt his face burn at how casually everyone spoke about this. If he could find a hole, he'd crawl in it. "What about the coronation? He's busy."

Malcolm flashed him a wide smile. "Who's getting crowned?"

CHAPTER 19

Casimir sat in his workroom cutting a new pattern for the coronation. His mind was buzzing with new ideas. Two days naked with Tucker had gotten his creative juices bubbling like they hadn't in years. It had also gotten him a bit behind, so he had to focus on getting things done.

The bell above the front door jingled and he sighed. He had an appointment with a couple who specifically requested him. Jotting down a few notes, he headed out to meet the customers.

He saw a man and a woman standing in the center of his shop, chins tilted up, gazing at his wares. He approached them. "Can I help you?"

Their interested gazes shifted to nervous stares. The man's face softened, but he looked apprehensive. The woman's face hardened and she had fire behind her eyes as she took a step forward and spoke in sharp clipped words. "Mr. Silk, I understand that you do more than design clothing. You also do event planning." It wasn't a question, but stated as a fact. Casimir felt that if he were to say no, she'd demand he change his answer.

"I do some types of events. What event were you hoping to hire me to help you with?"

Her eyes narrowed. "Our…child, they are eleven. We want to throw a coming out party for them. They have changed their name…as well as their gender. We want to have a celebration. We aren't sure how to do this, Mr. Silk. We weren't…we didn't…understand at first, but we do now. Can you help us?"

He thought about her request. He'd given up small parties, birthday parties, and celebrations for people under the age of twelve…but this was different. He would absolutely help a child who needed their community to support them. Every single time.

The bell tinkled again and another woman entered. A regular who came in for an outfit about once every week or two. Tabatha came in from the back to help fill her request.

"I believe I can help you with your event. If you'll step

over to my desk, we can get some details down. When will we be helping your child celebrate their true identity?"

Once he was done with the couple, he headed back to his work area. He started to lose himself in his work when his phone dinged with a text. He'd ignored his text messages for two days, but now he had to face the real world. As the owner of the business, he didn't have the luxury of ignoring messages.

With a sigh, he flipped over his phone and saw the text was from Malcolm. `Important meeting. Please come to the palace.`

He rubbed his forehead and sighed. "Tabatha, will you pack this all up? I don't know if they want a summary of my work, or what, but I'm being summoned to the palace again. Why did I agree to do this? I need coffee."

"On it, boss. And you agreed because not only are you the best, you wouldn't trust anyone else to work on your friend's wedding *or* crowning. Now, the wedding was a success. All you have left is to put a crown on him. Stop complaining; you know you love it all."

He laughed, shaking his head at her as he began to mentally form a checklist of what he needed.

It didn't take much time to get everything together and for him to drive back to the palace. He wondered how long it would take for him to have his own parking spot.

A servant led him to a conference room with Malcolm, Finley, and Prince Adrian. He set his portfolio on the table and took a seat. "I take it this isn't a meeting to discuss the coronation? Not without the Queen and her Advisor."

Malcolm's smile widened, something Casimir hadn't seen in weeks, outside of marrying Finley. "Oh, that's part of it, friend, but not in the way you're thinking. We've learned a bit of sibling history. We'll give you all of that later, but for now, we think our father's death was planned, not an accident as everyone thought. Due to the situation, we're worried about your safety. We'd like you to relocate to the palace until we get this all figured out."

Casimir narrowed his eyes at his friend, then cleared his face to look at the other Prince in the room. "You want me to move into the palace? For my safety?"

Prince Adrian cleared his throat. "It's a bit more complicated than that. The situation is highly confidential. We are hoping we can trust you with our secrets. Malcolm is convinced this is true. Is this true, Mr. Silk? Are you trustworthy?"

There was something in the way the youngest Prince spoke that sent chills down Casimir's spin. Something had happened, and for some reason, he was being brought in. "Why? Why would you tell me anything? I am nothing more than a simple designer."

Finley laughed. "There is nothing simple about you, sir,

but we have several reasons to want to trust you with this. Three I can think of off the top of my head."

Casimir rubbed his eyes. "Would I be held within the palace like a prisoner, or would I still be able to get my work done? I do have a thriving business beyond what all of you ask me to do."

Prince Adrian, whose face had stayed impassive, nodded. "You can head to your office each day, but I would request two things. One, you let Malcolm return to work with you, and two, you let me assign a security detail. If Malcolm works with you, no one will question the addition of palace security in and around your establishment."

A small thrill went through Casimir at the idea of getting Malcolm back, but his head began to hurt. He was missing something. "How are you going to explain the next King of Ixica working as an assistant at a fashion house?"

Prince Adrian's head tilted to the side. "And we are back to my original question, Mr. Silk: can we trust you?"

Everyone in the room seemed to hold their breath. Each face gazed at him with a different expression, but they were all serious…tense…stressed. This was not the time to dally or mess about. "Yes, Prince Adrian, I can be trusted. I will keep any secret you ask me to keep. I am loyal to the Royal family. Would you like me to sign a confidentiality agreement?"

The young Prince rubbed his face as if he'd feared a different answer. "Actually, I would." He slid a piece of paper over.

Casimir read it quickly. It stated that he'd keep all information covered in the following meeting and over the upcoming days confidential. Any leaks could and would result in imprisonment.

He didn't know what he'd gotten into or why, but realized something big was going on. Reaching into his bag, he pulled out a pen and signed the paper, then slid it back to Prince Adrian.

The young Prince signed the paper as well, pushing it to his brother before turning to Casimir. "Mr. Silk—"

"Please call me Casimir—unless you prefer formality."

He smiled. "Casimir, and please call me Adrian, unless my mom or Sidney are around. We recently learned two things. One is amazing news, one…not so amazing. Both will hopefully involve you. First, Lady Emma has agreed to marry me. We're planning a small ceremony…soon…very soon. Second, it appears I will be the next King of Ixica, not my brother. We need to adjust…well, you'll know best how much of the planning needs to be adjusted."

Casimir had a new appreciation for the idea of one's head exploding. *I disengage from the world for two days, and everything changes.* "I will happily help with both of these events, though I'm still uncertain why my relocation to the palace is necessary."

Malcolm grimaced at him. "Tucker is one of the lead people searching for the wanker who killed our…father.

He believes the person has been watching the palace. As soon as he determines we're on to him, he'll know that he and Finley are the two likely to try to track him down. We figure if he can find out secrets online, he'll know who our online experts are. If he decides to attack people close to them…well, you'll be right there at the top of the list."

Casimir looked down at his hands, thinking. "I could end things with him; would that help?"

Malcolm's voice came out soft. "Could you?"

Meeting his friend's eyes, Casimir thought long and hard about that simple question.

CHAPTER 20

Tucker lay on a towel next to the pool in the new swimsuit Emma had convinced him to buy before coming on this farce of a vacation. He was still tired after days lacking in sleep, or he'd have gone to the basement and run another simulation, maybe even done another training session with the staff he'd help hire into the job he wanted.

They kept asking him to show them how he'd run his defense against Finley. He wanted to wait until the system was better set up. Thinking about their duel still frustrated him. He knew he hadn't had a chance against the expert hacker and he only had spit and vinegar, but he'd hoped to last longer. He'd pulled out a few traps that usually tripped people up longer than the mere seconds it took that man to slash through them.

He'd never seen a hacker with the finesse and skill Finley possessed. He'd never failed to stop a hacker; he needed to go learn a bit more. If there were more out there like Finley, his office back in Chicago was in trouble.

They really didn't need Tucker when they already had an expert, and with him *not* becoming a King, Finley could devote his time to protecting the kingdom. They probably found a 'job' for Tucker to appease his friends…he really should just pack up and leave, it didn't make sense for him to stay. He should just tuck his proverbial tail and go.

His thoughts moved to Emma and her new duties. He laughed every time he thought about her starting up training to be Queen. God help them all!

His gut twisted and a wave of loneliness washed through him. Emma was going to become the Queen of Ixica. First it was going to be Jamie, not Emma. Emma was the better choice, if anyone were to ask him—not that anyone would. Deep down she wanted it, and she'd thrive in the position. She was perfect.

And Tucker? He'd go back to his office in the clouds overlooking Lake Michigan with its tan walls and the stock photo of the desert. At least the cactus in the photo had a tiny pink and white flower on it; not all of them did. It made it more homey.

He decided his choice to give in to the distraction of

Casimir had been the right one. It made this whole trip a bit lighter, and a lot more pleasurable. Despite his current lolly-gagging, he knew he'd be spending more time lost on the computers in the basement, and not much time with the sexy designer, so his two-day hiatus would be a nice memory to return to. The real vacation during his vacation.

The sun was getting brighter, so he stretched and covered his eyes with an arm. He debated a quick swim before he sucked it up and plugged into a computer for a few hours. Who would want to blackmail the King? How would they find him? He had a memory of a class…a professor…a goofy story…

A weight landed on his waist. He let his arm slide behind his head as he squinted up to see a tumble of brown curls and dark brown eyes. *Do not fall for this man, Tucker. Keep it light. Is that even possible? Is it too late? Can you go back to 'light'?*

He groaned as Casimir smiled suggestively, then the siren of a man dropped down and kissed him.

Casimir pushed up, settling lower on Tucker's hips. "I was informed I needed to relocate to the palace because of this bugaboo. Then they asked which rooms I wanted to bunk in…I requested your rooms, if that's okay with you."

A thread of desire spun from Tucker's lips down to his groin and he groaned at the thought of spending more time with Casimir.

CHAPTER 21

As Casimir straddled Tucker, he could feel the answer to his question as the man below him hardened at his words. He smiled as warmth filled him. Though confused as to why this man meant so much more to him than any of his other conquests, he decided it didn't matter. In a few days, maybe a week, he'd be on a plane to Chicago, and Casimir could go back to his own life. He could allow this slight obsession to continue in the meantime; it was perfectly safe, he told himself for the tenth time that day.

He took a moment to enjoy the pool area he'd designed. He thought back to that competition all those years ago; it was all here: the pool, the hot tub, the kitchenette. He looked over his shoulder. Even the sunroom had been part of his original design. He couldn't believe they'd really implemented all of it…this outdoor living spot was the start of him as he was today. The thought made him giddy. He wanted to share this with Tucker, his history and how his designs shaped his life, but then he remembered his time with the man was short because his days in Ixica were numbered.

Thinking of Tucker on a plane to Chicago caused another emotion within him, but Casimir decided to ignore it. It wasn't one he understood or could categorize and decided it probably didn't matter.

He leaned down and crossed his arms on Tucker's chest, rubbing his crotch against the other man's. Tucker's small whimper made him smile. "You know, I like your suit."

A mischievous smile blossomed on Tucker's face. "What little there is of it? If you don't stop wiggling, the damn thing won't be worth the money I paid for it."

"Hmmm," Casimir hummed. "That sounds like a challenge worth taking."

Tucker groaned again, squeezing his eyes shut. "You do realize anyone in the palace can see us right now. And with how you're sitting, I look naked."

"You, naked, I like the sound of that." He leaned down to Tucker's ear and gave it a quick lick. "We could move to the hot tub, then this—" he slowly shifted his hips left and right, "--won't get you in as much trouble."

Tucker took a ragged breath. "You're killing me. I don't know if I can get to the hot tub without flashing anyone watching…and do you even have a suit?"

One more lick, and then he nibbled the end of Tucker's ear. His whole body shuddered under him and Casimir smiled. He was having fun. "No, and if I have my way with you, you won't either."

"Anyone…you hear me, *anyone* can come out here. But…what do I need to do to get you naked? Here? My room? Just tell me."

They decided to head up to the room. Climbing off Tucker, Casimir saw the fancy suit hid nothing and didn't quite contain Tucker's arousal. Chuckling, he grabbed a towel and threw it at the other man. Tucker wrapped it around his waist, grabbed his clothes, and led the way to his room, locking the door behind them.

Once in his room, the towel and suit were quickly gone. "That is not comfortable when you're around," he complained.

Casimir laughed. "On the bed. Let's take care of your current state. I have work to do today; we can't spend the day in bed, though I do have some rules for sharing this room."

"Rules? This is my room! You have rules for *my* room?!"

Sliding Tucker's cock in his mouth, he sucked it in, then slowly moved it out. "Rule number one, when we're in the room for any length of time…no clothes."

Arms trembling, Tucker lifted up. "You're doing this now?

Casimir lifted a brow. "Do you agree?"

His eyes had gone wild as he scanned the room. "No clothes? Sure, whatever."

Casimir lowered his head and gave two more long strokes with his mouth. "Second rule. No one else while you're in Ixica. I've decided I don't share well."

Tucker's body trembled and he didn't try to lift up again. "Yes…okay…as long as it goes both ways."

Casimir reached down and clasped his balls before taking his pulsating cock in his mouth. He continued his rhythm, feeling Tucker's body tense. Then he pulled up. "No secrets. I know there'll be some things you can't share, but I'm here because of this thing…I want to know as much as you can tell me."

His whole body trembled. "Ah…. Gah…. Agreed." His voice sounded strained and breathy.

Casimir lowered himself to continue, enjoying both the action and the game. He thought of another question, but Tucker orgasmed and Casimir helped him to finish his waves of pleasure, almost coming himself.

CHAPTER 22

Always an early riser, Tucker enjoyed a few minutes of cuddling with Casimir each morning before starting his day. It soothed a part of him that would be missing his friends, having this man share his space. He never thought he'd enjoy it so much.

He quickly dressed and blew Casimir a kiss on his way out, though the man slept and would never know.

He thought about the different attempts they'd each tried at finding the trail to the person who'd blackmailed the old King, but that trail was dead…old, cold, and dead. There was no way to find it, much less follow it. He kept trying to remember that wacky teacher he had his sophomore year in college with the hare-brained challenges. Wasn't one of her challenges like this? *Why can't I remember her class?*

He'd been racking his brain trying to remember something that may help, but nothing had worked. Finley had been on the problem as well. He knew Finley was an excellent hacker, but didn't know how well the man could follow a dead trail.

They'd both worked with the new staff, not giving much details, just saying they were following an old trail. They hoped that within their training something would trigger a new thought and they'd figure out…anything really. There was also the hope that new minds would come up with a crazy idea that just might work. He and Finley were like sticks in the mug, so stuck in their ways. Maybe someone fresh and new would come up with a solution so fantastical that they would find their culprit.

Deciding it was time to get to work, he leaned over to kiss his lover. Casimir groaned, deepening the kiss. He smiled, then looked at the clock before pushing Tucker away. "God above, I hate you. Leave me to my beauty sleep!"

Tucker slipped into the walk-in closet and put on jeans and a t-shirt. The room was so damn big, his apartment in Chicago would fit inside it. He feared making a sound because it would probably echo almost like an echo-chamber.

He stopped by the family dining room for a breakfast

sandwich and a large mug of coffee, then headed down to the basement. His mind whirled around the idea of an echo-chamber as he dove into the code. Headset on and music playing, he circled the area where the blackmail documentation had been stored, where the hole had been found.

Imagining an old-timey flip book where each picture was a pinch different, and the faster you flipped the pages, the more animated the image got, he started to flip back, day by day, through the archives of the images of the site. He knew others had done it, but he wanted to go in fast-forward.

He wanted a larger overview of what happened in the area over time. He watched for microscopic differences. Something slight that would be easily missed unless you saw the animation that could only be seen in fast forward. He got to the end and started again flipping faster…and faster.

He began to wish he'd picked up the book with the juggling clown from his childhood instead—it would be more entertaining. *What the hell am I doing?* His head pounded with this tedious process.

The images blurred and took on the aspect of a negative imprint as he stepped further and further back in time. His eyes watered, and he squinted to focus, but he thought he saw a blip. He pulled up the bottom of his shirt to wipe his eyes and repeated the last few steps. The blip repeated…gotcha!

He took a second to first tense and then release all the stress in his muscles. He pulled up the correct timestamp.

The image was clear. Of course it was. If there were anything there, it would've been found a long time before this. He needed to find the path, the string, to follow.

What had the one professor said all those years ago… negative space! That was it. She had babbled on about looking for what wasn't there in the damned negative space.

He set up a filter on the code, and there it was, faint, but a path he could follow, like a wiry string. He felt an energy in his chest as he slowly followed the trail. His heart pounded faster, in time with the pain in his head…but if he stopped now he wasn't sure he'd find this again.

He tracked the code, slowly, quietly, trying to keep his motions on the web invisible. His fingers flew over his keyboard as fast as he'd ever typed, mocking the slowness of the progress he made following the path. If he moved too quickly, the hacker would find him and flee, wiping away the last remnants of the trail—what little there was of one.

Trembling with relief, he finally found the other end of the precarious thread. He took a quick snapshot of the IP address, taking over the camera for a hot second as he got an image of the person behind the screen, thankfully the person was doing something on his system. Before the person even noticed his invasion, he was out, gone like a ghost. He had the name, face, and address of the person they'd been looking for. All he had to do now was report this to Finley.

Falling back in his seat, he rubbed his eyes, body

shaking all over.

"How the hell did you do that?"

Tucker jerked and twisted to see the room full of people. Sitting next to him was Finley, gaping at him.

"You saw?"

Finley nodded. "Everyone saw; you were at it for hours. We set up the TV a few hours ago and tracked your progress. It was all recorded. But how the hell did you do all that? I swear nothing you did was possible."

Tucker opened his mouth then closed it. "I, ah…I don't know, I used echolocation and negative space…I guess."

Eyes furrowed, Finley's head tilted to the side. "Like a bat?"

Tucker laughed. "My head is pounding. Can I explain it later?" He picked up his cold coffee and realized he hadn't had more than a sip. It sat next to his untouched breakfast. "How long have you all been sitting here?"

"Long enough."

"Did you get it all? I grabbed screenshots if you didn't. Sent them to your phone."

His brows shot up as Finley dug in his pocket for his phone. He spent a few seconds looking before putting his phone away. "Email and text. So, you spent hours tracking a person down who was untrackable, then, at a critical moment where you could've been caught, you snagged pertinent information, photo, location, IP address, and sent it to my email and text just in case before covering your tracks and pulling out?"

"I also sent it to Adrian."

"Who the hell are you?"

Tucker shrugged. "Someone who is very hungry… and apparently someone not good enough to stop you. Though I did try."

Finley stood as he headed out the door. "I don't know about that. If we had a fair test, I'm not sure who would win."

CHAPTER 23

Tucker paced the room, naked. It was one of the rules, and he followed it admirably. It did make focusing on anything else a bit difficult, but Casimir felt it was worth it. Tucker rubbed his face. "I don't know what I'm doing. They said pack. Should I pack everything, or just for a few days? This is so frustrating."

"I still don't understand why they told you 'no' when you asked for a job. They utilize your skills…a lot. You're saving their ass. It seems to me they'd be in a lot of shit if you weren't here to save them."

Tucker turned to him, but before answering, his eyes

tracked up and down his body appreciatively. By the end, Tucker had grown hard and ready. The joy and curse of forced nudity.

Stepping up to the bed, Tucker crawled over Casimir until he hovered over him, their heads mere centimeters apart. "I can't think while in a room with you naked. This rule was created to keep me continually fucking you."

Arching up, Casimir purred, "Maybe I just like seeing you harden every time you look at me. We don't have to do anything…just seeing all your man flesh is enough."

He growled low in his throat. "Not for me." Tucker flipped him over and he felt the lube seconds before Tucker followed through with the treat of continued fucking.

Tucker finished his packing, got dressed, and left. He was part of the team going after the man who blackmailed the former King. Casimir wasn't thrilled, but he understood. Someone who understood computers had to go. The only other option was Finley, but he was a Royal now, and that would draw too much attention to the operation. They needed a ghost, an unknown. The only person with skills, security, and anonymity was Tucker.

Casimir made his way down to breakfast, ate, then headed to his shop. When he left, there hadn't been any security by his car, but he'd decided to leave anyway. He doubted from what Tucker had told him that the person was aware they'd found him or that he was in any danger. He arrived early, and got things going. An hour later, Malcolm showed up with his security contingency. "Casimir, why didn't you wait? You know we want you protected, too."

He shrugged. "I don't really think I'm in that much danger, and we're talking an hour. The lot of you have upset my life quite a bit. I just wanted an hour of quiet alone time. Not to mention, Princling, I can't open my shop as late as you get here. It's enough that I'm living in the palace; I can't change my hours, too."

The other man slumped in his seat. "I get it. Are you doing okay? Everything still okay with you and Tucker? I know the idea of this much time with one bloke must be twisting your mind."

Casimir sighed. He hadn't meant to snap at his friend. "Work. I'm sorry I'm acting so stressed. I'm fine. You continue with the coronation. I'm working on the wedding." He turned his back on his friend so he couldn't read his face.

He could feel Malcolm's gaze burning into him. "Are you worried about Tucker? He's with a bunch of security and they're going after one man. It should be fine."

"I know, but when this is all resolved, then what? He told me he requested a job with Finley and Adrian right at the start of all this. They never gave him an answer. He's scared to go back to Chicago alone." Casimir shook his head. "Forget it, I probably shouldn't have told you that. I'm talking to you as a friend, not a damn Royal. I just… he's been stressed. I think I'm his only outlet."

His friend put down his pencil, a shadow crossing over his face. "He has family back home, other friends, and his work."

Casimir gave him a bright smile. He'd always been an excellent actor. "Precisely. Now, these events your family requests won't plan themselves, and in two days is the renaming event for that other family. I'm very excited about that as well. Where do you want to start?"

CHAPTER 24

Tucker woke up in a small hotel room. The room boasted two queen sized-beds and they'd decided to double up in the rooms for safety. Two SUV trucks had brought six of them on this trip, so they had three rooms.

Tucker wanted to bang his head at the word 'job.' *What am I doing here? This isn't a game. Everyone else is armed, everyone but me. I'm part of their job, their responsibility. They have to keep me safe. It's all ridiculous!*

They were all paid members of the palace security. Members with the highest level of clearance. During the first day of travel he'd learned that all but one had parents who had served the palace in some capacity. One was even a third-generation member of the guard.

And me? I'm some schmuck who should be sitting by the pool drinking some fru-fru alcoholic drink before heading back to Chicago and my stupid-ass job. When I think of all the hope I had when I packed up my apartment and office…I'm just glad I didn't tell anyone about my plan before leaving. Then again, who would I have told?

With a sigh, he rolled from the bed and pulled on some clothes. In the bathroom, he washed his face and brushed his teeth. A free breakfast came with the price of the room, so he quietly left and headed down to get coffee and a bagel…or whatever it was they offered the weary traveler.

Once away from the dark room and the sleeping security, save the one that trailed him, he found the dining room, got his food, and sat. He turned on his phone and played around on social media. He had some work emails that he answered. It seemed it had been mostly quiet and they were surviving without him. There were a couple of emails asking when he'd get back, though. Without sending a reply, he left the email app, and pocketed his phone.

Across the room, a news report ran on the TV about the upcoming wedding between Emma and Adrian. Apparently that news had leaked. He quickly snapped an image of the headline and texted it to Emma and Jamie.

The newscasters went on to discuss how interesting that

all three siblings married so quickly. One of them leaned in to whisper that they heard that Princess Jamie was good friends with the woman Prince Adrian planned to marry.

"Do any of you know if Lord Finley is part of this friendship group? Maybe they came to the palace to woo the Royals!"

One of the others rolled their eyes. "Where have you been living? Master Finley, oops, Prince Finley now, and Prince Adrian have been friends for years! You can find pictures of them going back for ages. There is no connection with our British lord and the two Americans."

They continued to talk and make predictions, but Tucker tuned them out. Gossip about people he knew lacked any appeal. He saw his own image flash on the screen and blanched. *God above, this is awkward.* A man on the other side of the room gaped, looking back and forth between him and the image of him standing between Emma and Jamie at the beach. He had no idea where they'd found that picture.

He dropped his head into his hand and rubbed his face. *Well, at least when I return to Chicago, this will no longer be an issue.*

He heard rustling and looked up in time to see a few people around the room shift and stand, sights pinned on him. *Oh, shit! Are they really going to come talk to me? Is this a mob? Will they attack? What the hell do I do?*

Just as he was ready to run, two of the palace security

dropped down in chairs at his table. "It looks like our job just got a bit harder. Damn sleuth went digging, and you are no longer a nobody like us. Why don't you finish that up, or wrap it up, and we'll head out. The…ah…locals are getting restless."

The idea that people recognized him and wanted a piece of him made him tense. He wrapped up his bagel and drained his coffee. "Can we get more coffee on the road? Maybe get a pastry?"

Three security members had entered the dining hall and they all had their back to him, watching the crowd. Tucker walked to the door. One guard took a spot in front of him, another behind. The one in front grunted. "Yeah, we'll stop. None of us got food or coffee, and with this reaction, we don't want to eat here. Don't worry, we don't blame you. Someone leaked this, and their head is going to roll."

CHAPTER 25

Casimir and Tabatha spent an hour cleaning up the workroom in preparation for the two American Royals coming to the studio. The wedding was around the corner and the bride needed to have her dress fitted. Malcolm wasn't coming in because he was working with Adrian and Sidney to figure out who leaked the information about the wedding.

The room was cluttered, but his priority was getting Emma's dress hung in a place of honor. Casimir spun to Tabatha. "The women will be here soon, we have to be ready to wow them with our ideas."

Tabatha stopped her cleaning. "Are you really worried?

What has gotten into you? They've already seen the designs you've come up with. Lady Emma is so thrilled to be marrying her Prince, I think she'd walk down the aisle naked and still be happy. So, tell me, what is *wrong* with you?"

He fell into his normal seat. "Nothing, I'm just discombobulated. Having to live at the palace has messed up my routine. I'll be fine in a day or two when I can move home and shake everything off."

Tabatha's brow rose. "Yeah, I'm sure that's it." Her tone told him she didn't believe a word he'd uttered.

Casimir was about to ask what she meant when the bell above the door rang. Grumbling, he got up and met his customers. He smiled when he saw it was Jamie and Emma, and not someone else. He wasn't in the mood to interact with other customers today. "Morning, ladies, welcome to Ixica Couture."

Emma's eyes widened. "Can we skip the dress-fitting and just shop? These clothes are amazing! I haven't shopped in weeks."

Jamie grabbed her shoulders. "Give me a direction, stat. This is an emergency."

Casimir laughed and pointed toward his workshop.

Pushing her friend, Jamie mouthed, 'Thank you.'

They all headed into the back and the two women paused, gaping at the large room. The two rotated, taking in the designs, fabric, and Tabatha. Emma spoke first. "Oh, my God, this is all amazing. It's like being in the middle of one of those design competition shows, but so much better because these designs are breathtaking. I could faint right now. I just wish Tucker was here. Did he die when he saw this place? He loves watching those shows with us. Did he tell you he always predicts…like…everything on those shows? The judging, the winners, everything."

Jamie laughed and faced Casimir. "She does stop talking and lack of air won't make her faint…I don't think. I mean, she hasn't fainted yet. Tucker and I have timed her before on how long she can talk without stopping, but then we got bored." Emma reached over and slapped Jamie on the shoulder, but Jamie ignored her and continued. "She may ask you to supply her with outfits from today until forever, and I offer my condolences now."

Casimir had to bite his cheek. He could see why Tucker enjoyed these two women. They were fun. He suddenly realized they were the new Ixican Royalty, and that was fantastic. He also felt sadness for what Tucker would lose. "Can I call you two Jamie and Emma? That's how Tucker refers to you and it's how I find myself thinking of you. I can shift if you'd prefer…"

Jamie rolled her eyes. "Please…please just call me Jamie, and I love that you are entertaining Tucker. He is the most amazing person I know. I've been so busy, I felt awful when I realized how much time he would be alone after this one," she slapped Emma on the shoulder, "became joined at the hip with my brother-in-law."

Emma blushed, and it looked lovely on her. "I didn't mean for all this to happen so fast, but I love him. We've been talking since we met. I mean, I knew I'd be distracted, but I agree…I did Tucker wrong. We need to apologize to him. Especially me. I don't know how much of his past he's told you…but he shouldn't be left alone for too long, he gets up in his head…"

Casimir led Emma to the bridal dress, pointed to it and her, then pointed to the changing room. "If you're worried about him being alone, then what happens when he heads back to Chicago, alone?" His voice was low, concerned. He wasn't sure the two had thought about Tucker's future.

Both women paused, scrunched up their faces, and tilted their heads. If they'd planned it out, they couldn't have been more coordinated. Emma had lifted her hand to take the dress, but let it fall without touching the garment. "He isn't going to take the job in the palace?"

Dread filled Casimir. He wasn't sure if it was at the idea that Tucker *would* stay or *wouldn't. Do they not know he wasn't offered a job? Has no one told them?* He decided they had to know, they were Tucker's lifeline. "What job? Last I heard he asked but was never given an answer. He's been psyching himself up to go home alone and have only himself and his job left in that city of yours."

Jamie's hand shot to her mouth as her eyes grew to the size of saucers. "Oh no, I didn't know. And what about you? The two of you have grown so close."

"To be honest, I'm not the type for relationships; we only agreed to play knowing there was an end in sight."

As soon as the words left his mouth, a sadness filled him. He pushed the emotions aside; now wasn't the time to think about it. He had a career to worry about, and Tucker was off doing a job for the palace. He had enough stress worrying about that—not that he'd really admitted that to himself before this moment.

Emma's face hardened. She walked over, snatched the dress, and stormed off to the changing room.

From the changing room, Emma's voice came out muffled. "I plan to get this issue with Tucker and the job fixed, and when you break my brother's heart, I'll fix him... but designer boy, you are making the biggest mistake of your life...*damn it!* Jamie, get your ass in here, I need your help!"

CHAPTER 26

Tucker licked the chocolate off his fingers, then he finished his coffee. They were twenty minutes from the address he'd found for the man who'd been blackmailing the King, Henry Tort. The leader of the group decided to stop and discuss the plan…again. They wanted to rehash the details one more time, make sure all the pieces were crystal clear. Four of the five security members pulled him aside to warn him, "Look, we have guns. We don't know how dangerous this job will be. Let us do our job, go in, get this guy. Stay in the car until we give the all clear. Once we signal you, you can go in and do your thing, 'k?"

Each time, he'd smiled and nodded as if he hadn't known that as soon as they piled in the cars at the palace. "Sure, sounds great!" He wasn't sure how much of an idiot they thought he was or how idiotic their normal clientele were, but he tried to shrug it off.

When they got to the house, a fifth security officer tried to pull him out. "Come on, sir, it's time to head in." The other four melted into the shadows, already on course to their assigned spots.

Tucker didn't release his seat belt. "I'll wait until the leader comes and gets me, that's what several others told me. Those are the orders I was told to follow."

He shook his head. "New orders. You're to come with me. We're to enter in the rear. You know all about that, sir, right?"

Ignoring the jibe, Tucker stared at the man. He had been in the other car, so Tucker barely recognized him. Doubt and confusion warred in him over the order until the man held out his hand. "Hurry, we need to get into position, we're jeopardizing the others."

"What's your name?"

The man's face hardened. "I'm security officer Simmons."

With a sigh, Tucker released his belt and grabbed his bag. Simmons dragged him to a spot in the backyard to the side of the back door. "Stay here. Do not move until I come for you."

He could hear the sound of one of the security crew

whispering near him as he discussed everyone getting into position. There was a crash as the side door slammed open and then silence. Tucker squatted by the back door, under a window. The blood pounding in his ears made it hard to focus on anything, but he tried.

He tried to breathe slowly, but his insides tingled with fear. His mouth was dry and his hands shook. Simmons was long gone, and he felt completely exposed.

Shouts started up in the house. Each one made Tucker flinch as he imagined it as a gunshot, his brain having to translate the sound from a gun to a voice. He gave up trying to control his breathing.

Simmons came out. "Follow me. The computer room is clear."

"Have you captured the guy?" Tucker's voice came out wispy and low. He barely recognized it. Why had he walked into an active engagement? Why couldn't he just go back to the car and wait?

"Damn it, pretty boy. You're my responsibility, and I'm giving you an order. You have one job: clean up that damn computer. I'm telling you to move your ass now. If you get your part done, we can get our part done and leave."

Tucker's mind stuttered, but he didn't know what else to do. None of the other security staff were anywhere in sight. He straightened and Simmons grasped his arm, pulling him into the house.

They entered into a small kitchen. The sink was full of dirty dishes and the room smelled of rotting meat. He tried not to use his nose as his stomach rolled and tried to empty itself.

Another tug, and he was dragged down a hall and through a doorway into a dingy living room. There was a lamp on a side table with a dim glow emanating from it. Blinds covered the front window and a series of computers and monitors stood on a table against one wall. Simmons pushed him towards the setup. Tucker stumbled on the dirty brown rug.

"Get to work so we can get out of here." The disgust in his voice confused Tucker. He didn't know what he'd done to upset Simmons.

He sat at the computer and was glad to see they'd gotten in before Henry had time to lock anything down. With a shudder at the thought of touching the filthy keyboards, he tugged on gloves, and began typing. He pulled up the first window, and sank into the existing code.

Henry had several different entrances into the web and dark web. Tucker lost himself following his trail to different memory banks. Each locked with a different set of security codes.

Tucker disengaged and searched the desk, ignoring the sound of the security doing their job in the background. Plans had changed and he needed to focus.

He found a small notebook of codes. He tried each one,

and got into the first vault. He found a list of people's names with corresponding codes attached to each. He took a screen capture and sent that information to himself and Finley.

Henry Tort swore at the security detail, but Finley ignored it, that wasn't his responsibility.

The next path he followed was trickier; it had a few pitfalls. Circumnavigating the chain of steps took time, but if he went fast he wouldn't survive the game. He found the next memory box at the end and took a few minutes utilizing the codes from the desk drawer. None worked. He tried using the codes from the image he'd texted himself, and finally got in. More information. He copied it over to an external drive he'd brought along, destroyed the original, and moved on.

There were so many of these memory banks. Each one had a treacherous entrance sequence. Each one had a series of codes to enter. Some of the storage files were hidden once he found the end of the path. It took all Tucker's skill to find, copy, and destroy everything Henry Tort had amassed.

After the seventh vault, he heard the yelling and fighting again, but this time the sounds of the gun shots was unmistakable, but it had to be coming from the other side of the house. Security wouldn't have put him at risk. Screams and shooting. It was like living in his old neighborhood. White-hot pain blossomed in his hip.

Biting down hard, he tried to ignore it...he had to

finish what he'd started. There were eleven memory banks in all. He copied them each to his drive, burning down everything Henry had created. When he finished, he slipped his external drive into his bag, and slid to the floor, body shaking, his vision darkened.

More yells came from around him, but it didn't matter. He'd done what he needed to do. When someone touched his shoulder and moved him, he yelped. "Take the computers. Bring it all."

He wasn't sure if he'd made any sense, but that was the last thing he knew he had to say. Closing his eyes, he let himself rest. At this point, nothing else that happened to him mattered.

CHAPTER 27

Emma and Jamie were back to get adjustments made on Emma's dress. Casimir made the final adjustments and both she and Jamie swooned.

Jamie's eyes looked like a cartoon character's. "Oh, my God, Emma! If that isn't the most beautiful dress I've ever seen…. You look amazing. Adrian will faint dead away… he won't know what to do with himself."

Emma's eyes narrowed as she gazed at herself in the mirror, shifting left and right. "Good, that's what I want. I'll tell you this much, Mr. Silk, you are an amazing designer."

She'd refused to call him by his first name ever since

she'd learned he may be the instrument of harming 'her brother's' heart. He couldn't quite blame her. He could see how Tucker could earn such loyalty.

Jamie had changed into the bridesmaid's dress. "This will look good on both me and Anastasia."

Casimir's straightened, taking in a calming breath. "Anastasia? I thought Tucker was standing with you."

Emma's face hardened. "The Queen Emma requested a more traditional wedding this time, and having a female and male standing with me wouldn't be traditional. I debated only having Jamie, but agreed to two when Adrian said he'd have Tucker stand with him."

For today's fitting, they were only approving the design, not making the final adjustments. That would happen later when Anasatsia was here as well…and there was a second dress. The dress was cerulean blue with plum accents. The men would wear a darker blue suit with a light plum shirt and a matching tie.

Jamie poked Emma. "Okay, Ms. Queenie, off with the dress. We should head back and see if there are any updates from the stealth squad. They should've gotten to that man's house by now."

Casimir gazed at them. "Could I offer you a ride? I'd like an update as well." He could hear the stress in his voice, but thought he hid it well.

The women stared at each other for a moment, before

nodding. Emma shrugged. "That's fine. Riding with security gets old…fast. But we'll be surrounded by security."

They both changed back into street clothes and Casimir led them to his car. Back at the palace, they didn't even need to ask where to go. One of the servants saw them and immediately said, "This way. They're waiting for you in the main conference room."

Casimir's heart stopped. If everything had gone down, and they were done, wouldn't Tucker have texted him? On the way up the stairs, he pulled out his phone and checked. No text.

In the conference room, Malcolm, Finley, Anastasia, Adrian, and the Queen sat watching a speaker. They barely acknowledged their inclusion into the room. The three sat.

Finally, Emma said, "Can someone please tell us what's going on?"

Adrian wrapped an arm around her and sighed. "I'm sorry, we're all so on edge. The team went in with very strict orders. Secure the man, Henry Tort, then have Tucker go in and secure the computers. Easy-peasy. Well, getting the man out was a bit tricky. Apparently he locked himself into his room and began shooting. Two people were hit; both unconscious, one may not survive. That was the text we got. No names, no more information other than that. They can't give us much more; digital communication is tricky at best and can be hacked."

Emma's eyes had gotten wide. "Okay, that's bad. Really bad. Why do you all look like you've seen a ghost?"

Finley shook his head. "The operation started at ten this morning. Or about then. If this man locked himself in his room and there was a shootout, that means there was a bit of a complication. I received a text from Tucker with his first forays into Henry Tort's data at ten forty-five. That isn't late enough for the gun fight. We don't know why he was already working at that time. We don't know what happened."

Jamie's head jerked. "Tucker was in the house during the gun fight?"

Adrian shrugged. "We don't know. We're just guessing."

Casimir's world shrunk to the size of the room. It felt like he'd been beaten up. He actually thought he'd rather *be* beaten up. "Tucker may have been shot? He may not survive?"

He knew they all stared at him. Tears burned down his face. Something inside him was breaking, and he didn't understand any of it.

CHAPTER 28

Every bump the car went over made Tucker want to scream in pain. They'd given him a pill and said it would help, but their medicine was bullshit. His hip felt like he'd been shot…which he had been, and it hurt like hell.

After the head of security had found him and the medical lead had patched him up, there had been a discussion of taking him to the hospital.

"Am I going to die?"

He'd only gotten a grunt for a response."

Wanting to snarl, he asked again, "Am I going to die?"

The medical man glared at him. "No, and if you'd

listened to us, you wouldn't have been grazed by a bullet in the first place."

He sighed, the world turning on its axis. "Just take me back to the palace. If I'm stable, just…make things easy, please."

There were more grumblings, and a lot more glares, but he'd been dumped in the back of a car and they started the trek back home. He figured the only thing stopping the majority of security from giving him a piece of their minds for being where they hadn't expected him was that he'd been shot. He figured his time for a good verbal slap down was coming, he could see it in their eyes.

They decided to drive through the night to get him back to the palace. He wasn't sure of the time they'd driven because he kept passing out when they went over really big bumps. He tried not to complain. Another person on the team hadn't fared as well as him. He'd gotten shot in the lung and they'd dropped him off at a hospital.

Tucker wanted to get back to the palace and lie in his own bed. He wanted to sleep for a week. He wasn't sure if he cared about anything other than not bumping up and down in a car. He knew the security team had questions for him, it just hurt to think and talk, and Simmons kept glaring at him whenever anyone else asked anything.

A jolt of the car woke him up. The sky was dark, and the tinted windows didn't allow him to see any stars or the moon. The car was eerily quiet. Patting down his pockets, he found his phone. He carefully pulled it out and sent a text to Finley. Don't trust Simmons. Brought me through house early. Talk when I return. T.

His phone said it was three in the morning and he bit back a groan. He didn't want to be up this early, but wasn't sure he could sleep. A reply text came back almost instantly. You okay friend?

He thought about the communication available, and realized the people back at the palace may not know everything that had happened. He knew his phone had more protections than most, but also knew he was now in the public eye. Mostly. Won't be dancing. Probably a good thing, with my skills.

There was a bit of a pause before the reply came. There are many here who are glad to know you're safe, dancing or not. We'll see you soon, friend.

Being called "friend" almost made him cry. He knew then he should sleep, but he'd slept a lot, and the pain was too much. There wasn't anyone awake to give him one of the inefficient pills…probably a placebo.

He managed to slip his phone back in his pocket before croaking out. "Are we there yet?"

A head in the middle seat popped up. It was Simmons. "Close. A couple more hours." He spoke a bit louder. "I don't know why you demanded to get out of the car and go into the house like you did…really put us all in danger."

Tucker glared at the man, and he sneered back. He turned in his seat and sat with his back to Tucker.

The SUV hit another bump and he grunted in pain. Lightly touching his hip, he felt a tacky stickiness and wondered how much more blood he'd lost during this drive.

When the vehicle finally stopped, the pounding in his hip competed with the drum solo in his head. He felt nauseous and hoped he made it out of the car before anything happened. Although, if he could plan to throw up on Simmons, he would happily arrange that.

The doors opened and the driver pointed a gun at Simmons. Simmons's smirk morphed into a snarl as his body jerked.

"Don't go for your gun, Simmons. There are three of us. You won't survive." The voice came from outside the SUV.

Simmons shifted his focus to the back seat. "Maybe I'll have enough time to take him out with me. Then you won't have the information you so desperately want."

"Think about this, what have you done so far? Been an ass, went against orders, endangered a civilian and an operation. If you make a move, it'll be much worse."

"First they were going to let a queer have the crown,

not to mention an American. That got fixed to being just a queer. But now we're back to an American. Did you hear me, man? They're going to let an American have one of *our* Ixican crowns." Simmons started to breathe more heavily.

The man outside the SUV was speaking patiently. "What does it matter? We always bring in a foreigner for the marriage. It ensures a healthy royal line."

Simmons glanced at Tucker then at the man outside the SUV. "They're going to ruin our country. Why don't you understand?" He lunged for the man outside the SUV, but a crack told Tucker he didn't get far.

Tucker closed his eyes and really wanted to throw up. After a few minutes, a couple of people helped him from the SUV onto a stretcher. The contraption bumped a few times, and the jarring was just too much. He leaned over the side and emptied his stomach. Someone handed him some water and he rinsed out his mouth.

He felt himself lifted and then he was inside the palace. He closed his eyes and ignored everything, waiting for sounds and motion to stop. When he finally stopped moving, he moaned in relief. A cool washcloth wiped his forehead and cold metal pressed on his side. He tried to see what was happening, but the hand on his forehead held him down.

"What are you doing?" Tucker's voice was thin and soft.

A heavenly voice answered, "They're cutting off your pants to see your wound."

Tucker cracked open his eyes to see Casimir standing above him. "What are you doing here?"

Leaning down, he gave Tucker a quick kiss. "My heart almost stopped when I thought you may not return. I've been waiting for you…. I…I don't know. I can't leave. Not until I know you're okay."

"Of course I'm okay. You're too busy to be here. You should go. Maybe see me tonight?" He shut his eyes tight as the pain radiated through him.

A light kiss landed on his cheek. "I'm not leaving until you stop making those painful faces. It hurts too much… in here." He tapped Tucker's chest. "So, stop complaining and let me be."

His head started to swim. He wondered if they'd slipped him some drugs. He tried to say more, but wasn't sure if Casimir understood. "Thanks for being here. Feels better with you here."

CHAPTER 29

Casimir spooned Tucker in bed. He'd been returned to him just over a day ago. They needed to be careful. The bullet had dug a groove just above his hip bone, causing a lot of blood loss but no internal injuries. The doctor had advised no strenuous activity for the better part of a week. They were both trying to be good.

He thought back on the last few days, and all he knew was he'd come face to face with losing Tucker, and he didn't like it. Tucker had promised him as long as he stayed in Ixica they'd be an exclusive item, and he planned on holding Tucker to that…no matter what. Something in him shifted.

The wedding was later that day, and the two of them needed to prepare. Tucker was in the wedding party and had to be ready to walk down the aisle. They couldn't do anything that would jeopardize his mobility.

With a groan, Tucker rolled to his back. "I want to play. I have the sexiest man ever in my bed…and nothing." His face scrunched up and he lightly touched his bandaged hip. He took a deep breath as his body relaxed into its new position.

Casimir leaned down and gave him a deep kiss, savoring the taste of this man he'd come to…he shot up and gaped at Tucker. A warmth infused him as he gazed at this man.

Tucker's brows came together and his head tilted. "What? Did I do something? Did you forget something? Did you suddenly decide we should attend naked…some new wedding fad? Because I don't think I can do that. You can convince me to do a lot of things, but that may be a bit much for me." He laughed, ignoring the pain.

Casimir opened his mouth to answer, then shut it and smiled. "I swear to you, we are doing another few days where we're naked the whole time, but not until you're able to keep up with me. But no, you naked is only for my enjoyment, I already told you that." He leaned down for another quick kiss. "Now, if you'll stop distracting me with all this 'naked' talk." He growled low in his throat to emphasize his point.

Tucker rolled his eyes. "We are naked. How can *talk* of

being naked be more distracting?" His warm hand lifted to stroke Casimir's side.

Taking his time, Casimir let his eyes wander down the length of Tucker's body and then back up. "Valid point. My imagination is not better than the real thing. Your body is just spectacular. Maybe if you stay in just this position…"

"We tried that last night. It was glorious, right until it wasn't. Three more days and I should be better. Maybe if we broke rule number one and just wore loose pants?" With a laugh, Tucker moved his hand to Casimir's cheek.

Casimir narrowed his eyes. "Never! That is a very important rule. If we're to cohabitate, that rule is a must. As for the other rules…well they're important, too. Now, can I get on with what I wanted to say before you so rudely distracted me with all your 'naked' talk and naked…nakedness?"

"Of course. Proceed, sexy man."

Casimir leaned down for one more quick kiss, and then he placed his forehead against Tucker's, their faces centimeters apart. "Tucker Black…I love you."

CHAPTER 30

Tucker gazed up into the dark brown eyes above him and felt like he could melt. "You've had my heart for a while, sexy man. I just couldn't tell you…I was afraid I'd lose you."

Casimir resumed the kiss, tongue exploring, tasting, feeling. Tucker felt like his world could end right then and he'd be the happiest he'd ever been. His hands explored Casimir's body from memory, knowing every supple curve and hard plane, yet he hungered for it as if he'd never touched it. He stopped himself from grasping his cock and starting something they couldn't finish—not here, not now. He groaned in desire.

The other man pulled away, a small smile on his face. "I'm glad I'm not the only one suffering right now. Let's get you dressed. You need to be ready to stand up with Adrian when he marries your sister."

They dragged themselves from the comfortable bed and to the shower. They dressed and headed down for breakfast. Tucker went to make sure the grand ballroom was prepared for the wedding, and Casimir ran up to help the women with their dresses.

Tucker began directing staff on every aspect of preparation, like an orchestra conductor. From flowers to chairs, floor coverings to wall coverings. There was a list, and like a good elf, he checked it twice, leaning on a stylized cane to help him stay up.

"Tucker, can we talk with you?" He spun to see Finley and Adrian in the doorway. His hip hurt from standing so long and he hobbled to the door to meet up with them.

Behind them stood Malcolm, who held out his hand. "I'll take that, if you don't mind."

Tucker handed Malcolm the notebook of wedding prep and followed the other two men into the throne room. Adrian grabbed a chair for him. "We'd head up to a conference room, but you look ready to fall over. You push yourself too much, my friend. Rule number one, take breaks and care for yourself."

He scrunched up his face. "What is it with you

Ixicans and your rules?"

Adrian tilted his head. "What do you mean?"

Tucker shook his head, his face warming. "Nothing. Let's back up a step. Why are you giving me rules?"

Finley smiled. "It's my fault. You asked for a job in the middle of my training…I had a lot of things going on. I thought I had said 'yes, a thousand times, yes.' You started working, doing the job I thought we'd agreed on, training, being utterly brilliant. I figured we'd do that paperwork later. Then Adrian came up to me, telling me how upset Emma was that you were leaving, having never been offered a job. Every time we asked you to do something, you never once even questioned it; you just did it."

Grabbing another chair, Adrian sat. "I don't get it. You were asked to do more than just about anyone these last few weeks…. Why didn't you ask for the job again, or remind us?"

Tucker shrugged. "Americans are known for being pushy…I didn't want that reputation. You two said you needed to discuss it with the Queen, I figured that's what you were doing. I don't know what all needed to be decided."

"And you would've just gotten on a plane and returned to Chicago?"

He slumped. "Probably. It would've killed me, but I'm not good at being places I'm not wanted. I spent my childhood being unwanted. It isn't something I ever want to repeat."

Finley put his hand on Tucker's knee. "Is that what you think? That we didn't want you around?"

Tucker took in a big breath and let it out. "Such an odd discussion before the wedding. Yes and no. I was spiraling. Emma and Jamie are all I have, and knowing I was losing them caused me to lose my mind a bit. I wasn't thinking straight, except when I was in the code. It's the real reason you kept finding me in the basement. It was the only time I felt grounded…well, until I connected with Casimir…but you probably don't need those details." His face warmed more.

Both men smirked. Finally, Finley shook his head. "I'm good at what I do, but so are you. I think the two of us together can create something no one can digitally penetrate. I want to learn how you found that wanker— who is in jail, if no one told you. So is Simmons. He was the one who leaked the information about the wedding. He was trying to make things harder for the Royal family, but I think things may be easier now."

Adrian leaned back in his chair. "The wedding is today, mum is thrilled. The coronation will be in a month or so and Emma will be an amazing Queen."

Tucker smiled. "You have no idea."

CHAPTER 31

Casimir and Tucker lay in the tiny bed of Casimir's flat. Though it had been several days, the bandage on Tucker's hip reminded Casimir of the night he spent in the conference room, not knowing Tucker's fate.

Everyone sat, waiting for news, but all they'd heard was one of the security members had been dropped off at the emergency room. His condition was stable, but the doctors wanted to keep him for a few days for observations.

At eleven at night, Finley turned to Casimir, face grim. "You don't have to wait. We'll come and get you if we hear anything."

It had sounded logical, but he couldn't get his body to move. Frozen in place, body tense with worry, he licked his lips, and his voice came out quietly, with a desperate edge. "What if Tucker texts me? Maybe I should stay."

Casimir shifted his focus to Malcolm, who looked at him with a knowing glint in his eye. "Yeah, my friend, that makes sense."

The text hadn't come to his phone, but he couldn't have moved from that room before knowing Tucker's fate. Hearing what the text said, he worried more about the man he now knew he loved. When they finally brought Tucker in, he only had eyes for Casimir, something settled in him.

He leaned down and gave Tucker a kiss, his heart full with this new emotion…love. He never thought he'd want this or needed it. Now he couldn't imagine living without it.

The wedding had been two days ago, and like the last wedding he'd planned, they'd spent the days following it together at his flat, alone…and naked. Unlike the last time, they had to be careful because of Tucker's injury. Despite that, it had been time well spent.

Today they planned on opening a bank account since

Tucker had received his first pay check for the work he'd been doing at the palace. They would find a restaurant for breakfast first…but Tucker had been quiet since they'd woken up. Casimir suddenly wondered if he was too quiet.

Casimir rolled over and lay on top of him, enjoying how well their bodies fit together. "What's wrong?"

Tucker quirked a half-smile and very quietly said, "I love you."

Warmth infused his body as it had every time Tucker had said those words and his body hardened. "I love you, too."

His gray eyes deepened almost to a slate and he bit his bottom lip. "You are such a free loving spirit…I don't want to presume…but I love sharing space with you, and I even love your crazy-ass rules." His hands rubbed down Casimir's back. "But…now that I'm being paid…do you want me to find my own place?"

Pressure built behind Casimir's breastbone as he froze, poised over the man he loved. So much had changed within and around him. *What do I want? He is offering me an out to put my life back to the way it was before. I've always maintained I never wanted anything serious. And he wouldn't be out of my life if he wasn't living here. We'd just have more space, a bit of separation.* Something constricted in him at that thought…a weird tightness in his chest.

He stared around his tiny flat, barely big enough for him and his stuff. Could two people live here and not end up killing each other? Would their relationship...did he just think that word...was he okay with that word? Would it survive such tight quarters?

He tucked in, cuddling with the man who'd taken his heart—blended their souls together—and sighed. Could he imagine not having this every day?

"I think you should look for a flat...something bigger than this."Tucker froze under him as he sucked in a breath. Casimir leaned down to kiss him before continuing. "Something big enough for both of us and our stuff... something we can call ours."

EPILOGUE

Tucker dug in the refrigerator, looking for something to eat. He and Casimir had lived in this new apartment…flat…for over a month, and he still couldn't believe it. So many changes so fast.

When Tucker and Casimir had looked for a flat, the Royal family made it clear it had to be large enough to accommodate all of them for a meal or hanging out.

The dining room had a beautiful light oak table that sat ten. The Queen herself had gifted it to them as a flat-warming gift. It came with a matching buffet. The kitchen was standard and the flat had two bedrooms and two bathrooms, a public one, and an ensuite in the master bedroom.

The master bedroom was about as big as Casimir's old flat, which wasn't that much smaller than Tucker's old place in Chicago.

During their search, Tucker and Casimir had found a few places they'd thought were good. Tucker had gone out with Emma and Jamie, and they'd liked the places, too. But then Adrian, Malcolm, and Anastasia got involved. They explained that as friends of the Queen—both current and future—they'd need more space.

When they'd moved in, they'd both been a bit overwhelmed at the size of the place. Neither of them had enough furniture to fill the space, even with Tucker's stuff from Chicago. A series of flat-warming gifts—along with dipping into the money each of them had been saving— had created a new space that was all their own.

Tucker loved it. He'd never felt so at home.

All of Casimir's focus had been on the set up for the Royal coronation taking place tomorrow. Tucker convinced him he needed some down time, so they'd taken the morning off to play, and Tucker needed calories.

A knock at the door had him popping up like a prairie dog in a field. Tucker's head snapped towards the sound, before he shut the fridge and ran to the bedroom. He let his eyes scorch over the perfect, naked man in the bed. "We need to discuss this rule of yours. Now that we're living together, are you really going to insist on 'naked all the time'?"

Tucker fought to search for clothes instead of jumping on Casimir.

Casimir chuckled low and seductively, not moving from his spot. "Oh, yes, this is the most important rule." He let out a low hum. "Your shirt is on the chair by the closet, love."

Hoping to get his foot into his black slacks, Tucker finally got the pants—trousers…gah, stupid words—on. He slipped on a thin, gray v-neck sweater. "Do I care about my hair?"

"Always, but you look fine. I'd fuck you."

Tucker snorted. The knocking at the door came again, and he jogged over to check the peephole. "It's Royalty. You may want to get dressed."

A grumble was the only response.

Tucker opened the door and smiled at his bosses. "Hi, Fin, hi, Malcolm. To what do we owe the pleasure of your company? Hiding from the insanity of the palace?"

They both smiled mischievously as Tucker waved them in. The door opened to a large living/dining area. The living room featured two large couches and two armchairs.

Finley and Malcom walked to the living room and sat on one of the couches. Tucker took the couch perpendicular to it. "So, to what do we owe the pleasure of your company?"

Malcolm leaned forward. "We wanted to invite you and Casimir to the palace to have a celebratory dinner with the Queen tonight. It's her last night with the crown. Then you could take a guest room and be there in the morning to help set up."

Casimir came out from the hallway, impeccable as always: charcoal slacks, light gray button down, each hair in place. *How the hell does he do that so fast?* He sauntered over and sat next to Tucker, resting his hand on Tucker's leg. "Give up our day alone to hang out with you lot?" He sighed dramatically. "Well, I guess after the coronation we'll have a day off for good behavior." He squeezed Tucker's leg as he said the words.

The side of Malcolm's mouth quirked up. "Oh, I know, dining with the Royals, so very difficult. But, considering everyone in the palace is a bit insane right now, how about we hang out a bit here before heading back into that insanity?"

The look of hope on Finley's face made Tucker snort. "That bad?"

Finley just nodded. "Insanity. Getting the back garden ready for all the people who want to watch…the cameras, the…well, everything. It's utter madness."

Tucker woke up early the next morning. He kissed Casimir gently before unwinding from the beautiful man. In the bathroom, he freshened up and located his clothes to wear for the coronation. He quietly slipped out of their room to find coffee.

In the family dining room, he found Emma and Jamie. He ran in as they leapt up, and the three hugged. They'd all seen each other the day before, but not alone, not like old times, not just the three of them.

"So, my receptionist sister, you're now going to have to organize a whole country...I don't know if Ixica knows what they've gotten," Tucker said, giving Emma an extra squeeze.

She laughed. "I can't believe at the end of the day I'm going to be the Queen...of a country. I mean, when it was Jamie, I was all about it, but...me?"

Jamie snorted. "Oh, no, I think that this makes *way* more sense."

"Me, too," Tucker agreed. "I can't think of anyone I'd trust, curse, whatever, with this position over you."

They all laughed as coffee appeared at the table and they all took their seats.

Emma sighed. "So, how is the new flat? With 'Queen school' I just haven't had the time to get you alone. Casimir is always around. Talk."

Warmth filled him. "I never knew. When we lived in Chicago, I got into a rut. I don't even think I realized how much of one. I tried to swallow my emotions, make myself robotic, but it wasn't working."

Both women snorted. Jamie said, "I don't know

who you thought you were fooling. It's nice to see you happier, my friend."

Before they could talk more about their past, the Queen came in. "Oh, I'm usually the first one here. Good morning."

They all started to stand, but her raised brow kept them seated.

"Today I go back to being just Rebecca. It will be so nice."

Emma laughed. "You'll never be *just* Rebecca, you know that. But I'm glad you can be in a bit of a less stressful position."

Tucker sat next to Casimir. "Is this what you envisioned when you designed the coronation?"

Casimir's eyes drifted over the people, the stage, the Royal family on the stage, and a dreamy smile crossed his face. "Yeah, it is."

Queen Rebecca stood at the center of the stage, facing the crowd and cameras. "Today begins a new chapter for Ixica. I believe it will be one of our best ever. My son, Prince Adrian, has shown himself to be caring, brilliant at leading people, and knowledgeable in the rules of our land. Lady Emma, hailing from America, has impressed and inspired me in the time I've known her. I believe each and every one of you will come to love her as I have. She is smart, caring, and has each and every one of your interests in the forefront of her priorities. She will be a Queen of Queens, representing Ixica as well as any I know."

As the Queen moved to a table with the crowns, applause exploded from the crowd. The Queen smiled while Adrian and Emma tried to keep blank faces. Adrian did a better job. The layers of official garb helped to hide the trembling Emma must have been experiencing.

A smile tugged at his mouth, pride swelling in him. *I'm so proud of her.* He took a tissue from a pocket and wiped his eyes. Casimir's warm hand reached over and squeezed his thigh.

The Queen took the crown from the table, and carried it to Adrian. "Prince Adrian, with this crown, I pronounce you King Adrian, the twelfth King of Ixica." She then moved to the table and took the second crown and moved to Emma. "Lady Emma, with this crown, I pronounce you Queen Emma, the twelfth Queen of Ixica."

Tucker looked over at Casimir, excited for his friends and their new Royal lives, hopeful for the country's future, and mostly he was very much in love with the man next to him. Casimir smiled and leaned over and whispered, "Finally!" Before giving him a kiss.

Please review to help other readers know to enjoy The Royal Entanglement Series!

If you missed book 1 or the prequel, find them below:

Book 1: Finley's and Malcolm's story: Royal by Design:
https://mybook.to/RoyalByDesign
If you missed Jamie and Anastasia's story, find it here in
The Royal Ring: https://mybook.to/RoyalRing

Find more information on my website:
https://hannahwillow217.wordpress.com

Find me on:
Facebook
TikTok
Instagram
Twitter

ACKNOWLEDGEMENTS

The Royal Series has been a fun series to write. Once again, my original plans ideas were brought into focus by a trio of brilliant people: Wes Imrisek, Elizabeth Daly, and Angela Grimes. They read my words, and find ways to make them shine. Other people help to support and encourage me, the Confused Chaos writer's group, they are there every day, being snarky and clever. The group wouldn't be there if it weren't for the brilliance of C.C. Davies as she writes up a storm. Marleen Dekker and Kelsey Ortiz are the best beta readers ever. Fe Foster, Eva, Brian, Grant, Jacinta, Chris, and Nikki are always there to help to refine my thoughts and ideas, making me a better storyteller. My son is always there to help me brainstorm new and crazy ideas as are the rest of my family when I suddenly ask off the wall questions.

I want to thank all my family, friends, and any of you who are fans of my writing. I love creating stories, and plan on doing this for as long as you want to read about my crazy characters and their lives.